"Your father you'd marry Dr. Ellis."

Slade's words seemed to demand some kind of a reply.

Kimberley dropped into the nearest chair. "Yes," she said. "But I would never have married the doctor—I like him too much."

"Thanks for nothing," said Slade with sarcastic charm. "It's nice to know where I stand."

"Oh, you know what I mean! We hadn't known each other very long before we married—a divorce won't affect either of us emotionally, will it? Whereas, having known the doctor longer... and if, as you say, he's in love with me —" she looked away as she added "—well, I just couldn't divorce him could I? I'd be...."

"Stuck with him?" Slade finished for her. When she nodded without looking at him, he inquired blandly, "And what makes you think, dear Kimberley, that you aren't stuck with me?"

Dishonest Woman

by

JESSICA STEELE

Harlequin Books

TORONTO • LONDON • LOS ANGELES • AMSTERDAM
SYDNEY • HAMBURG • PARIS • STOCKHOLM • ATHENS • TOKYO

Original hardcover edition published in 1982
by Mills & Boon Limited

ISBN 0-373-02502-5

Harlequin Romance first edition September 1982

CHAPTER ONE

SUMMER came late that year. Kimberley Adams stood at the french windows of the living room that sunny September day, and sighed. She supposed she had better get a move on, otherwise she was going to be late for her appointment.

But she felt no urgency to leave Bramcote, the home she so loved. It was a long time since she had felt any urgency to do anything. She was alone now. Thank God she had Bramcote. Bramcote couldn't be taken away from her like everything else she loved.

It was maybe because she was so attached to her home, so used to it, that Kimberley did not see that there was a good deal not right with it. Her father had mentioned in February, when the roof had shown signs of deterioration after the heavy weight of snow had cleared, that they should put their heads together to think up a way to get some repairs done. But that had been just before his illness had struck. After that she was too concerned for him to worry whether the roof was sound or not.

She couldn't bear to live anywhere else, she thought, loving the isolation of Bramcote too, which only by virtue of the fact it was linked by a long lane did it manage to be included in the village of Amberton.

She gazed out at the long lawns that fronted the house, resenting that she had to leave for the, in her view, unnecessary trip into the nearby town of Thaxly.

Looking to the right of the lawns she saw the orchard where as a child she had whiled away many a happy hour—and wanted that happiness back with her. She sighed again as without effort the memory was with her that it had been there in the orchard that David had proposed. There that day he had sworn his undy-

ing love. She had been excited then, she remembered.
She had laughed as they raced indoors to tell her father
they were engaged.

Her thoughts back with her father, tears came to her
eyes, tears that were no stranger to her. She controlled
the feeling of wanting to collapse in a bout of weeping.
She had better get going. Charles Forester, her father's
solicitor, had telephoned three times for her to go and
see him. Though why he couldn't tell her over the
phone why he wanted to see her she couldn't imagine—or why he couldn't put in a letter what it was
all about without her having to traipse all the way into
Thaxly.

Kimberley couldn't think that anything he had to
say could be that important anyway. Bramcote, the
house she had been born in, loved almost as much as
she loved her father and David, was hers now her
father had gone. It was the only thing that kept her
sane, she had thought in her most despairing moments,
the knowledge that she was secure, safe, within the
walls of Bramcote. Whatever happened Bramcote was
hers, and if Charles Forester, who was old enough to
have retired years ago, wanted her to trail into see him
just to tell her that her father had left her very little in
the way of money, then she could save herself a trip,
because she already knew that. But money didn't
matter—Bramcote was all that mattered.

Two hours later Kimberley was back in the living
room of the home she loved—back, but not staring out
from the french windows as she had been before. She
was sitting in the chair into which she had half collapsed half an hour before, still stunned by what the solicitor had told her, his words going round and round in
her head. And still she couldn't believe them.

She had been in shock when after the preliminaries
he had got down to telling her the contents of her
father's will—so shocked she had been deaf to his ex-
pressions of regret. She had seen his mouth moving

without properly hearing him saying that the will was
so tightly sewn up that she hadn't an earthly chance of
contesting its contents.

'Would—would you repeat that again—the relevant
parts?' she had interrupted him, coming out of her dazed
condition to be certain he must have made a mistake.

'The money your father left you . . .' he began to
oblige.

'No, not that—I know it's only sufficient to keep me
ticking over. That part isn't important. It's Bramcote.
Tell me again my father's instructions about the house.'

The elderly solicitor had coughed twice, a sure sign
that he felt uncomfortable. Had he heard that she had
at one time been near to a nervous breakdown? she
wondered. Did he think she was going to throw a
screaming fit in his office?

There was compassion in his voice when he said,
'There's only one way in which you're able to inherit
Bramcote.' And he had then repeated what he had said
before, only she hadn't believed her ears then, and
didn't want to believe them now, as he told her, 'And that
way is if, on the date six months from the date of your
father's death, your status is that of a married woman.'

The sound of the telephone ringing intruded on that
phrase of Charles Forester's that was spinning round
in her head. She didn't want to answer the telephone,
didn't want to talk to anyone.

But the caller was persistent. Whoever it was was
determined to get her to answer it. Shut up, shut up!
she wanted to scream at it, the sound shrieking at her
nerve ends. But common sense prevailed. There was
only one way she was going to quieten it.

She left her chair and picked up the offending instru-
ment. Her voice lifeless, she gave the Amberton number.

'I've brought you in from the garden?' The voice was
one she knew—Doreen Gilbert, known in the village as a
helping hand to waifs and strays, a young-forty lady
whom Kimberley had known for years, and liked.

'It's nice out,' she said, going along with Doreen's assumption that her call had brought her in from the bottom of the garden.

'How are you?' was Doreen's next question.

'Fine,' Kimberley responded automatically—and wanting her to think she thought her enquiry was just a courtesy, and not because she might think she spent all her time sitting brooding, she offered the courtesy back. 'How are you and Edward?' she enquired.

'The same as we were two days ago when I last spoke with you over the phone,' Doreen replied, then got down to the point of her call. 'You know I told you then that I'd managed to persuade that spouse of mine to take an extended holiday.'

Vaguely Kimberley remembered. 'You're going to the Canaries, aren't you? Er—a week on Saturday.'

'Close,' said Doreen, a chuckle in her voice. 'Bahamas, actually, though you've got the date right. But it wasn't until last night that Edward reminded me it was my birthday the day before we leave—sadistic pig!—I told him I wasn't having another one after I'd clocked up forty. Anyway, why I'm ringing is that we've decided to have a party—nothing formal—I'll have my best dresses packed anyway.'

At one time this comment would have amused Kimberley, for Doreen's wardrobe was full to overflowing, adored as she was by her banker husband, what she spent on clothes never was quibbled at.

'I'm sure it will be a lovely party,' she offered, having attended one of the Gilberts' parties over a year ago with David, the party, with its unlikely mixture of Doreen's waifs and strays and a smattering of Edward's banking friends, going with a bang.

'I hope so. Now you will come, won't you?' said Doreen, going quickly on just as though she knew Kimberley was ready to back away from any such invite. 'Please, Kim, do come! It will spoil my evening if you don't. I worry about you rattling around in that old house all by yourself.'

'There's nothing the matter with Bramcote.' Kimberley came back straight away in defence of the house she loved, though without the heat with which she would once have defended it. Perhaps a lick of paint here and there wouldn't hurt, but . . .

'Now don't take offence. It was just a figure of speech,' Doreen came in promptly. 'I swear Bramcote is the love of your life, no man . . . Oh hell,' she broke off, obviously remembering Kimberley had once been engaged to David Bennet and the effect it had had on her when he had broken the engagement. 'Look, Kim, I'm going. All I'm doing here is putting my foot in it. The party is a week on Friday—just remember I shall expect you to be there.'

Kimberley came away from the phone feeling slightly peeved. Certainly not in the banking class, she wondered if she came under the heading of waif and stray. She didn't want to be one of Doreen Gilbert's good causes. She hadn't been to a party since she had received that letter from David . . .

'Oh, Dad!' she cried out loud, and sank down into his favourite chair again, wishing with all her heart he hadn't thought it necessary to do what he had. She couldn't bear to lose Bramcote. It was her home, her haven.

She knew why he had done what he had, of course. Up until ten months ago she had been the happiest of engaged girls, eagerly looking forward to her marriage in a month's time. Then that letter had come from David—a letter so out of the blue when his letter only a week previously had been full of words of love and how he was looking forward to their wedding.

The look on her face as she read his letter, the colour draining from her face before the tears had started, had alerted her father to the fact that this wasn't one of the usual letters from her Army captain fiancé.

'What . . .?' he had started to question, seeing the pain in her eyes.

Wordlessly she had handed him her letter for him to read for himself that David had met and fallen in love with someone else.

Her father had done his best to comfort her, but she had been too distraught to be comforted. Selwyn Adams, a mild-tempered academic, had then turned bitterly against David, had shown the anger she had been too devastated to feel.

'An officer and a gentleman!' he had snorted furiously. 'A gentleman would have come and told you personally, not written rubbish like this!'

'He—he probably couldn't get leave,' Kimberley had put in; loving David still as she did, it was second nature to defend him.

Weeks she didn't want to remember had followed. Weeks where nothing mattered any more. Weeks of her not eating, growing thin and listless. Weeks that had ended up with her father calling in a doctor to see her.

Not that Dr Ellis had been able to do much other than prescribe a load of tablets she didn't want, but which, seeing how distressed her father had become at her refusal to take them, she had downed, more to please him than for any good he or Dr Ellis thought they would do her.

How good her father had been to her in those early days of her having her love thrown back unwanted! He had talked to her for hours on end—though those talks had always ended the same way; with her vowing and declaring she would never marry. Her heart still belonged to David, and for all her father saying she would fall in love again, she knew she wouldn't. She didn't want to. Never did she want to feel this same emotion for another man—to sit anxiously waiting for him to arrive, to sit by the phone waiting for it to ring, to get as far as arranging the wedding only to find that there was something about her that made it easy for a man to fall out of love with her.

Kimberley left her chair and went to stand by the french windows. She couldn't give Bramcote up, she couldn't, she inwardly cried against the fact that she must if she didn't comply with the terms of her father's will.

Oh, how wrong he was to have made such a stipulation! Hadn't he understood that she could make a life for herself living here on her own? It was his way of trying to protect her, the way he always had, she saw that. He had known he was dying. Must have thought for her to have a husband would be a way of that protection continuing even after his death.

Bitterly disappointed, but loving her father too much to blame him for what he had done, Kimberley recalled one of their conversations shortly after she had left school, when after much debate it had been decided she should stay at home and run the house.

She had been in the village store when some chance remark about how like her mother she was, with her corn-blonde hair and hazel eyes, had brought forward the comment that she was less highly strung than her mother.

'Was my mother highly strung?' she asked when she had got home and put her shopping basket down.

'Talk in the village?' her father had asked.

And when she had told him what had taken place, he had told her what had led up to her mother's death, and the weight that had been on his conscience ever since. She had known her mother had accidentally drowned, and she still believed it was accidental when he had finished. But she saw then that it had been since her mother's death that her father had grown so over-protective with their ten-year-old offspring.

'Your mother and I seldom quarrelled,' he had told her. 'She was a beautiful woman, in ways as well as looks. But yes, she was highly strung. We were happy, Kim, don't ever doubt that. But——' he paused, then went away for the moment from the hazel-eyed girl with her corn-coloured hair flowing down her back.

'But you quarrelled about something?' Kimberley asked, sensitive to his every nuance.

'Yes, we quarrelled.'

'What about?'

He hesitated, looked at her, then told her, 'About you.'

'About me?'

'You were such a gentle little thing—cried if you so much as stepped on a spider. I thought it best for you to be sent away to boarding school. I thought it would—toughen you up a bit.'

Had he thought she resembled her mother in temperament as, according to that lady in the village, she resembled her in looks? she could remember thinking. Had he thought that she too was highly strung? Was that why he thought she should be sent away to be toughened up?

Kimberley remembered her unhappiness at the boarding school she had been sent away to. But that particular unhappiness had not lasted long. After a week she was back home again—home to stay. She had never returned to that school, for during her absence her mother had died.

'Your mother was most unhappy after you left. Not one smile could I get out of her the whole of those first dreadful days. Then one day she said she was going for a walk. Nothing unusual about that, she often went for a walk. But it was while she was away that I decided if you, who were so like your mother, were as unhappy as she was, then, having made my stand, I should bring you home again. I made up my mind to tell Rosemary this when she came in—only . . .'

Kimberley saw there were tears in his eyes that he was manfully trying to hold back. 'Only she didn't come in,' she said huskily. And tears were in her eyes too as she left her chair and put her arms around him. And, knowing him so well, knowing what was in his mind, 'She didn't commit suicide because she was so unhappy, Dad, I know she didn't. She loved you too much for that, loved us both.'

Kimberley still believed her mother's death was the accident it was said to be, but when David had thrown her over she had caught her father's eyes on her several times, just as though he was wondering if she too in her unhappiness would one day soon tell him she was going for a walk—and not come back.

But as unhappy as she was at that time, ending her life deliberately or accidentally was not in Kimberley's mind. Though it was to take several months before something happened that made her alert to the fact that not only had she lost the one man she loved, but that soon she was to lose the only other man she cared about.

Six months later, after an illness that had brought him pain and grieved her to see how each new day brought a further worsening in him, her father had died.

Kimberley got up the next morning after her visit to the solicitor, her mind still in turmoil that in a little over five months she was to lose Bramcote to some obscure charity her father must have pulled out of the hat, for she had never heard of it.

Without enthusiasm she set about her chores, knowing the day had to be filled somehow. She didn't want company, but she happened to glance out of the window and saw Dr Ellis coming up the path.

He had been kind to her, she thought as she pushed an escaping strand of silky hair back into the knot in which she wore it. He had lightly kissed her cheek as a sort of condolence on the day of the funeral. He had wanted to be kind to her that day, she knew, when he had suggested she call him by his first name.

There was nothing wrong in calling him by his first name, she thought fleetingly as she went to the door to let him in. He couldn't be much more than ten years older than her twenty years. But as she had known him as Dr Ellis since he had taken over the village practice a year previously, his christian name didn't roll easily off her tongue.

'Good morning, Dr Ellis,' she said, opening the door.

'Colin,' he said. And, comfortable with her first name, even when she didn't comply and use his, 'How are you, Kimberley?'

'Fine, thanks,' she said, and, remembering his kindness to her father, 'Have you time for a coffee?'

He followed her into the kitchen, but it didn't annoy her even though she had been meaning to deposit him in the living room. Very little annoyed her these days—nothing seemed worth getting stewed up over. The only thing important to her now was her beautiful Bramcote, she thought wistfully, and she was soon to lose it. It would be like losing her lifeline.

'I expect you're as busy as ever,' she remarked when they were sitting in the kitchen drinking coffee.

'If I say no then ten to one there'll be an outbreak of 'flu in the village,' Colin Ellis smiled, his experienced eyes noting the dark shadows under her eyes. 'How are you sleeping?'

Kimberley shrugged. 'All right,' she lied, beginning to regret her offer of coffee if he was going to turn this brief break in his busy morning into a discussion on her health, although that must be his reason for calling.

'You're still taking the tablets I gave you?'

She held back on the lie that would have been easier, and an innate honesty in her had her answering, 'When I feel the need for one.'

Dr Ellis didn't take her to task, not that she knew if it would have bothered her if he had. Though he did press, 'You still have a supply?'

She nodded, searching her mind for something to get him off the subject. She looked out of the window and saw it was another sunny day. 'Do you think it will last? The Indian summer, I mean.'

'You should get out more.'

Kimberley sighed. 'I might sit out in the garden this afternoon.'

'You don't think you should socialise a little?' he suggested.

'My father has only been dead two weeks,' she replied flatly, no anger in her statement.

'I know,' he said sympathetically. 'And you nursed him without sparing yourself. But it's over now, Kimberley. You've earned the right to begin enjoying life again.'

Kimberley wanted to be alone. She had had enough company for one day. She left her chair, taking her cup and placing it on the draining board, wishing she had left her remark about Colin Ellis being busy until now. Maybe he would have taken it for a hint.

He stood up. 'Are you going to Doreen Gilbert's birthday party?' he enquired, coming to stand near her.

Her innate honesty was discarded without conscience. 'I might,' she lied. It was easier to lie. She had no intention of going.

'I shall look forward to seeing you there,' he said.

Kimberley moved from the draining board to go and collect his cup. 'Yes,' she said, and was glad when he went.

She dismissed him and the party from her mind when he had gone. Then after rinsing the coffee cups, she did go into the garden, thoughts of her father, his will, and David filling her mind.

She thought constantly of all three in the week that followed, and found her face wet with tears many times. She cried easily these days, she thought, and sought hard to find some stiffening in her that would have her back to the laughing girl she had been twelve months ago. But that only led back to thoughts of David. He had been her world then, and more tears started. She no longer had David, no longer had her father, and soon—soon she would no longer have Bramcote.

It was on the Friday of Doreen Gilbert's party when, since the sun was still miraculously shining, Kimberley was tidying up the garden, when she heard the garden gate open. She turned her head, then straightened and stood passively watching as she recognised Doreen herself coming up the garden path, that 'I won't take no for an answer' look in her eye she had seen there when in the past she had gone round the village with her collecting for some good cause or other.

'Garden looks nice,' Doreen remarked.

'It's a full-time job,' Kimberley fenced warily.

'I could send my gardener over to give you a hand,' Doreen offered with her natural warm generosity.

'I like doing it—thanks just the same, though, Doreen.' And because Doreen wasn't moving, and because she liked her, 'Fancy a cup of tea?'

'Thought you'd never ask,' was the grinning reply.

It was over a cup of tea that Doreen came to the point of her visit. 'Got your dress pressed for tonight?' She made it sound like a throwaway question, but Kimberley knew her too well to be taken in.

She took a deep breath, wishing she would leave her to lead her life the way she wanted. 'I—er—Don't be offended, please, but I . . .'

'Don't say you're not coming!' Doreen got in before she could say just that. 'Oh, please, Kim! I've set my heart on you being there.'

'You'll have crowds of other people there. You won't miss me.'

'I will,' Doreen insisted. 'I've counted on you being there. Besides . . .' she broke off.

'Besides what?' Kimberley asked.

'It will do you good to get out,' Doreen said.

As Kimberley was about to say she was quite happy staying in, it struck her that Dr Ellis had said much the same thing. 'Have you been talking to Dr Ellis?' she asked suspiciously.

'Can you blame me if I have?' Kimberley saw concern in the grey eyes of her friend. 'We're worried about you, Kim. You're as thin as a stick, no colour in your face.'

'There's no need . . .'

'Please come, Kim,' she was interrupted. 'It will absolutely ruin my holiday if you don't come tonight.'

'Oh, really!' Kimberley scoffed, thinking, even with Doreen being Doreen, that was going over the top.

'I mean it, Kim,' she said, and sounded so convincing that Kimberley's sensitivities were pulled.

Would it matter so very much if she gave up an hour to put in an appearance at the party? Not that she believed she would spoil anyone's holiday if she didn't show. But—but Doreen did look worried about her.

'Do you never not get your own way?' she grumbled.

'You'll come?' Delight was beginning to show.

'You could charm the birds off the trees,' Kimberley told her.

But she was already beginning to regret her promise as Doreen Gilbert swung off happily down her garden path.

Later that evening, having already discarded one dress that hung on her where it had once fitted, Kimberley reached in her wardrobe for another, one with a tie belt and loose lines that wouldn't show her thinness up too much. Not that she was so scraggy, she thought without much interest as she surveyed herself in her full-length mirror. She had always had a good bust and still couldn't be mistaken for one of the male sex.

Who wanted to be fat anyway? she thought, as she dressed her long corn-blonde hair into a more becoming style than she usually wore it. And anyway, didn't she have more important things to worry about? Oh, how could she bear to give up Bramcote?

It was half past nine when she set off to walk the half mile to the Gilberts' substantial residence. Since she had no intention of staying longer than an hour, and since Doreen's parties usually went on from eight until all hours, she thought her timing was just about right.

The sound of beat music met her ears as she walked up the drive, making her want to turn tail and return to her quiet haven. But remembering the promise Doreen had extracted from her, she made herself go forward. The assortment of cars on the drive, from bangers to Bentleys, told her the Gilberts' guests would be dressed in anything from jeans to dinner jackets, and that she need not have bothered what she wore.

A manservant let her in, smiling when he saw who it was. 'May I say how pleased I am to see you, Miss Adams,' he said, which she thought was sweet of him.

'It's a thrash in there, is it, George?' she asked, knowing from a discussion she had had with him ages ago that the din blaring out fell painfully on his musical ear.

'I think everyone is having a good time,' he said diplomatically, a shade pompously, so that Kimberley came near to smiling.

'Kim, you made it!' Doreen came hurrying up to her.

'Happy birthday,' said Kimberley. 'I forgot this afternoon.'

Doreen shrugged it away, saying, 'I was just about to send a search party for you. But you did promise.' They were moving towards the drawing room, the music temporarily suspended while someone changed the tape, though the room was still lively from a healthy buzz of many conversations.

'I'll get you a drink, then introduce you round to anyone you don't know,' said Doreen, and was off before Kimberley could tell her she wasn't fussed about a drink or meeting anyone.

As she was on the point of giving herself a lecture, that she must make some effort seeing she had accepted the invitation at all, her eyes flicked round the room, without difficulty being able to file away which were Doreen's friends and which were the friends of her banker husband. The tubby, bald-headed man with his well cut suit had to be a banker, she thought. Her eyes lighted on Doreen, who had been held up in conversation with an arty type of about the same age as herself in check shirt and jeans.

She had just recognised someone from the village whom she knew, her eyes searching to see if Dr Ellis had arrived, when a tall man somewhere in his mid-thirties strolled in through the open balcony doors. Idly he glanced her way, then his look rested on her, and he stopped dead, his glance fixed.

Kimberley looked away, having registered in her own glance that his fine black sweater suited his broad shoulders, his athletic-looking physique telling her he never sat behind a desk all day. She dubbed the fair-haired man as one of Doreen's friends, and was then ready to forget him.

Only it wasn't that easy. 'We haven't been introduced,' said a deep-toned, totally masculine voice to the side of her.

Kimberley half turned, and looked up. It was the fair-haired man, who had just come in from the balcony. Probably he had been out there to cool off after dancing—or for some other reason, she thought, a painful memory digging into her of herself and David going out on to that same balcony because they had wanted to be alone.

'No—we haven't,' she said, her voice cool as she tried to surmount the pain of her thoughts.

'Slade Darville,' he introduced himself, his eyes narrowing at her coolness.

She wanted to be by herself; she wished he would go away. 'Kimberley Adams,' she replied, and while his hand came up to shake hands, 'Excuse me,' she said abruptly, and turned, not wanting him or anyone else to see she was battling against tears that never again would she go on that balcony with David.

She had herself under control by the time she had found Doreen, the idea in her mind to invent some excuse for going home. She had been rude to that man Slade whatever he called himself, and should stay around if only to apologise, but—oh, what the hell? He looked the type who could take a snub without breaking out into spots. Though, as a faint memory teased her of the narrow-eyed scrutiny he had favoured her with—he just wasn't used to anyone snubbing him, she felt she knew that for a fact.

'Here you are,' said Doreen, raising her voice slightly, since the music had started up again. 'Sorry I was so long—you know how it is.'

Kimberley took the glass she offered, realising she would have to make some pretence of drinking some of it at least before she made her departure.

'Now,' said Doreen, her voice back to normal since someone had turned the sound down to more bearable proportions, 'let's see, who would you like to meet first?'

Kimberley tried to show interest and glanced about, her eyes taking in the floor where she observed that the man she had snubbed hadn't been mortally wounded, if the way he was getting on with the redhead he was dancing with was anything to go by.

'Oh no,' said Doreen, her gaze following Kimberley's and seeing where her gaze had rested. 'Definitely not Slade Darville. He's not in your league, love.'

'My league?' Kimberley queried.

'He eats little girls like you for breakfast.'

'Big bad wolf?'

'More—rake first class, with gold stars,' said

Doreen—though she wasn't above sending a smile his way when the subject of their conversation chose just that moment to look away from his partner and straight at them, just as though he knew they were there and were talking about him. His glance fell away as his partner, seeing she didn't have his undivided attention, said something to draw his attention back to herself.

'There's no need for you to introduce him,' Kimberley said, a spark of mischief stirring itself for the first time in many a long day. And at the question in Doreen's eyes, 'He introduced himself.'

'Well, thank God he didn't follow it up,' said Doreen. 'You'd never be able to handle him if he felt like chasing you, love.'

Kimberley didn't think, much as her friend was warning her off Slade Darville, that she would appreciate it if she told her she had snubbed one of the guests in her house.

'You're saying I might find myself in deep water?' She didn't know why she asked the question. The subject had been as good as finished with. She certainly wasn't interested in him. She wasn't interested in any man—only David.

Doreen looked at her as though she too was surprised at her question, as though the last man she wanted her to show an interest in was the fair-haired man.

'Leave him strictly alone,' she advised.

'Why?' Kimberley found herself persisting. For although he had a certain air about him, a certain indefinable something, strictly speaking he wasn't all that good-looking. Now David . . .

'Because,' said Doreen, watching, as was Kimberley, the way when the dance tune finished, Slade Darville somehow extricated himself from the redhead, and now had a most attractive brunette in his arms, 'Because, that's why. He's strictly a pick-them-up-and-then-drop-them type. Even marriage wouldn't hold him. Now if you want to get involved with someone . . .'

'I don't,' said Kimberley sharply. Then, afraid her tone might have caused offence, she said, just for something to say to be friends again, 'Is he married?'

'No, never has been,' said Doreen, unoffended. 'Prefers to play the field, does our Slade.' She laughed lightly as a thought occurred to her. 'Though I'd like to bet if anyone *was* ever cute enough to catch him in a weak moment and did manage to get him to the altar, it wouldn't last after the first flush of romance had gone.' Kimberley heard the definite note of conviction in her voice as she went on, 'Once he realised what he'd done, I've no doubt at all he'd be off to his lawyers *tout de suite* getting the quickest divorce on record!'

So he didn't want to be married either, Kimberley thought, getting bored with him as a conversation piece, though if David . . . She snatched her mind away from David, wondering if that wound would ever heal. Then from nowhere something akin to excitement, dormant for so long she was barely able to recognise it as such, began to stir in her. She didn't want to marry unless it was David, and yet if she didn't want to lose Bramcote, according to her father's will, she had to be married in just over five months' time. Slade Darville must have felt some small pull of attraction towards her, or why else had he come up and introduced himself?

She looked towards the dancing area, some semblance of an idea trying to force itself on her. She couldn't see the man she was looking for. Probably out on the balcony with that brunette, she thought, not allowing thoughts of David that wanted to intrude come in this time.

'Er—you're sure he would apply for a divorce, once he'd realised he'd tied himself up to one specific female?' she asked casually, the idea in her head already dimming since she wasn't the type to go chasing after a man, and after her snub, he would have to be really interested—if only briefly, as Doreen had suggested was his habit—to risk another.

'I'd lay a month's housekeeping on it,' said Doreen without hesitation.

Kimberley thought it definitely was time to change the conversation. 'Dr Ellis said he was coming, but I haven't seen him.'

'Haven't you heard? There's some nasty tummy bug going round the village,' Doreen informed her. 'Poor Colin, he's helping out at another practice too because of staffing difficulties. He'll be run off his feet, poor lamb. Thank goodness Edward and I are going away. With luck, we'll miss the tummy bug.'

Doreen seemed quite content to stay chatting with her. But Kimberley was starting to get a conscience about hogging her hostess's company for so long, and said so. But Doreen would not move on until she was doubly assured by her that there was no need for her to introduce her to anyone, and that she would be quite all right on her own.

Kimberley stayed where she was after her hostess had gone. Glancing round the room, she decided to give it only a few more minutes and then go home. Slade Darville was still nowhere to be seen, and she designated the ridiculous idea that had come to her about him to the rubbish basket. He was probably much more interested in the brunette he had been with than he would ever be in her any way, she thought, wondering why once wasn't enough. Hadn't David shown her she wasn't woman enough to sustain a man's interest for very long? Three months was as long as their engagement had lasted.

Her engagement had not been the only thing to get broken—with it had broken all confidence in herself. And yet, fleetingly, the notion had flipped through her mind to try to get Slade Darville hooked long enough for him to marry her, and so save Bramcote from being taken from her.

Doreen was the other side of the room, Edward not

far from his wife. They wouldn't notice if she went home now, she thought. She could leave a message with the manservant George, as she went out.

Kimberley turned in the direction of the door, then stopped. Her way was blocked. She raised an unsmiling face past the black sweater that confronted her, and met blue eyes that were almost navy. She had in her sights the fair-haired man she had had that crazy idea about, and she lowered her eyes.

'You're not going home before you've given yourself the pleasure of dancing with me, are you?' enquired a voice she might have remembered had it not held a new note, a mocking note.

How he knew it had been in her mind to go home, she didn't know. What she did know was that, although she had never felt less like dancing, that crazy idea was back with her, making her stay, when what she should be doing was brushing past him and carrying out her intention of going home. The words Doreen had spoken, the conviction with which she had said them, were ringing in her ears, cementing her feet to the ground when she knew Slade Darville was more than she could handle—he'd be off to his lawyers getting the quickest divorce on record once the first flush of romance had gone—wasn't that what Doreen had said?

Without haste, Kimberley raised her large hazel eyes, her face solemn. Then for the first time in an age, her mouth, that had forgotten how to smile, slowly took on a definite upward curve.

'You too could be in for a treat,' she told the man she had it on good authority would run a mile from marriage—and ten to get out of it.

CHAPTER TWO

WITH Slade Darville's arm about her, the tape having moved on to a slow smoochy number, Kimberley felt more like crying than smiling. David had been the last person she had danced with, and just the memory of him made her feel unfaithful that not only was she dancing with someone else, but that she had so much as actually contemplated marrying someone else.

Slade Darville was a good dancer, holding her neither too loosely nor too tightly, and she liked that. But it was about the only thing she did like about him; she felt suffocated by thoughts of David, of losing Bramcote.

She wasn't short, but the man she was dancing with was taller than her by about six or seven inches. He had been chatty to his other partners too, she remembered. But with her he appeared quite content to circle the floor unspeaking.

His grip tightened when someone nearly cannoned into them, and Kimberley felt stifled for a moment until his hold returned to the firm hold it had been as he guided her clear.

She began to relax, seeing her notion to get him to marry and divorce her had been born in panic at the thought of losing Bramcote. By the very fact that he was making no attempt at conversation it was obvious he was the sort who thought, having accepted Doreen's invitation, he was honour bound to dance with anyone who stood about looking like a wallflower.

'What sort of work do you do?' came blurting from her in a burst of reawakening dead pride that anyone should presume to take pity on her.

Her head lifted with her question, meeting dark blue

eyes full on. She looked away when he didn't answer her question. Had she dropped a brick? she wondered, remembering she had already neatly placed him as one of Doreen's waifs and strays.

'Or perhaps,' she said stiffly, forcing herself to continue, 'perhaps you're without employment?' Many people she knew were unemployed through no fault of their own, and she wished then her second question had not sounded so accusing. It could have been that he hadn't replied because her question had embarrassed him.

She returned her gaze to him, her expression gentle, then saw a slow smile break from him. 'I'm having a rest from work at the moment,' he told her, and left her to draw her own conclusions from that.

The tune had changed while they were dancing, but if Slade Darville was just performing the politeness of a duty dance, then he made no move to escort her back to where he had found her as another smoochy number followed.

Silence reigned again between them, and Kimberley was glad of it as she felt that excitement surge in her once more that perhaps she hadn't got it wrong, that perhaps he did feel some attraction for her. The idea she had had before of keeping Bramcote through him was there again. And this time it wouldn't go away.

He had said he was having a rest from work. Did that mean he was an actor? Weren't actors said to be resting when they were without a job? She fell into deep thought, barely aware that her footsteps were following his lead as she wondered, if he wasn't all that interested in her after all, and with his reputation he'd be steering clear of marriage anyway, if she could find sufficient nerve to offer him a part to play for a very brief run. Her father hadn't left her very much in the way of money, but she would willingly give him half.

'That was perfect,' said Slade Darville from somewhere above her head. She looked up, too deeply involved with her thoughts to know what was perfect. 'The music has stopped,' he hinted.

Kimberley moved out of his arms. 'Er—thank you,' she muttered quietly, then found his hand beneath her elbow as he guided her back to the spot from where he had collected her.

She just wasn't up to this game, Kimberley knew it as she crossed the floor with him, her mind a blank as to what she said now to hold his interest.

'Was I right in assuming you were having thoughts of going home?' he asked as they halted, their way temporarily blocked by a knot of people.

'Yes,' she answered, realising she should have said no, if he was to be made to believe she in turn felt some slight attraction for him, that being the reason she had changed her mind.

'Then perhaps I might be permitted to escort you,' he suggested.

She didn't want him to take her home, didn't want him or any man performing that office but David. She checked. What did it matter what she did, who took her home? She was going to lose her beloved Bramcote, her refuge, if she didn't buck her ideas up.

'It—It's half a mile—and . . . and I prefer to walk,' she said—unsure of herself, unsure of him, unsure of how she would handle it if he owned one of the old bangers out there and taking her home suddenly made a detour or whatever technique he used.

'It's a nice night,' he replied, taking her answer for assent. 'Did you bring a wrap?'

She had handed George her woollen stole when she had come in, but she looked round to say goodnight to Doreen and Edward before she left the drawing room. She couldn't see them, and thought then as they went out into the hall that perhaps it was as well. She didn't want Doreen reeling back in horror after having warned her against Slade Darville when she saw just who was taking her home.

The way to Bramcote included the long narrow lane, pitch black at night, which she hadn't given thought to simply because on her own the darkness of the lane had never bothered her. But she was nervous now, with Slade Darville close beside her as they walked, the rake he was said to be in the forefront of her mind, she expected any moment to be pounced on.

But he was more sophisticated than that, she discovered, when once clear of the lane he had made no move to make a grab for her. In fact, she thought, nowhere near to getting to the bottom of him, he seemed disinclined to do anything but talk, ask questions.

'Have you recently moved to the village?' he asked.

'No,' she replied, and realising if her aim was to be achieved then she had better start saying more than solitary syllables to him, 'Why do you ask?'

'I've been to a couple of the Gilberts' parties recently. I should have remembered you had you been there.'

That sounded promising. It was the reason for the stirring inside her, she knew. 'I've lived in Amberton all my life,' she said.

'But you don't normally go to parties?' He sounded as though he didn't believe it. It nettled her, when little had annoyed her of late.

'My father—has been ill, and I've been nursing him,' she brought out stiffly, haltingly.

'I trust he's now well again.'

'He—died three weeks ago.'

'You're missing him.' His voice had changed, was gentle. It had tears coming near to the surface.

'Yes, I'm missing him,' she said, swallowing hard.

They had reached Bramcote, but she didn't want to invite him in. David had always come in for coffee as a right. She stopped at the gate.

'This is where I live,' she said, and couldn't help that her voice sounded wooden at the dreadful thought that Slade Darville, in the absence of an invitation for coffee, might think the least reward he deserved for the half-mile walk was a kiss. She didn't want him to kiss her, but if she was to play this out to the full, didn't she have to go through the pretence of seeming to be attracted to him? She gritted her teeth as she braved herself to accept his kiss.

'You live here all alone?' he queried, his arms coming nowhere near her as he observed that there wasn't a light to be seen anywhere in the house.

'Yes.'

'In that case the coffee you were going to offer me will have to wait for another time,' he remarked, skittling her belief that with his reputation he would be clapping his hands that he had a clear field, with no one to interrupt them. And while she had no reply to make as she wondered if this was a technique individual to him, or had things changed so much since she had dropped out of circulation, he was saying, 'I am going to see you again, aren't I?'

He's going to kiss me now, she thought, bracing herself, forcing herself to play her part. 'I'd like that,' she said.

He came forward, and Kimberley made herself stand still. But all he did was to bend down and unlatch the gate. 'I'll give you a ring,' he said casually—and had barely waited to close the gate once she was through the other side when he was going back the way they had come.

Kimberley was annoyed again as she went up the path and went indoors. He hadn't kissed her, made a pass at her at all! And his 'I'll give you a ring' sounded as enthusiastic as someone anticipating a painful extraction at the dentist. He hadn't so much as asked her telephone number.

He wouldn't be ringing, she knew that as she sat at the kitchen table, a warm drink in front of her that she had no idea why she had made because she didn't want it. Somehow during that half mile walk home Slade Darville had gone off her—if he had fancied her at all.

Her thoughts went to David and how soon his avowed undying love for her had evaporated. His defection had shaken her, had fractured any belief in herself that had grown from having him love her. It had left her with little faith that she could hold any man.

Slade Darville's attitude didn't help. It had her realising that at the most, an hour was as long as she was likely to sustain any man's interest.

Kimberley wiped away traces of tears as she stood up. She might as well go to bed. Better take one of her tablets too, she thought, her nerves feeling more shot than usual.

She was going along the hall when the phone rang. She flicked a glance at her watch, saw it wasn't yet eleven, wondered about taking the call in her bedroom, then nipped to the phone in the living room because it was nearer.

'Are you alone?' was Doreen Gilbert's prompt and agitated enquiry.

About to reply, 'Who would I be with?' Kimberley realised the reason for the call. 'You saw me leave with Slade Darville?'

'Didn't you hear anything of what I said?' Doreen came back. 'Are you all right? He made a pass at you, didn't he? Kim . . .'

'I'm fine, Doreen, stop worrying,' Kimberley cut her off.

And while Doreen came back to repeat a lot of what she had said about Slade's love-them-and-leave-them policy at the party, Kimberley fell to wondering if she would have felt better than she did at this precise moment if he had made a pass at her. At least it would have proved she wasn't totally lacking in some sort of attraction. Her brow furrowed at that as she pondered why it should particularly bother her, since before she had met Slade Darville she hadn't wanted any man to be attracted to her anyway.

On the point of deciding that it was solely because her idea for holding on to Bramcote was now down the drain since she had seen the last of him, she came out of her thoughts to hear Doreen asking if she would be seeing him again.

'No, definitely not,' she said, and knew it for a fact. 'Stop worrying, Doreen, do! All he did was see me home. He didn't wait longer than it took for me to get through the gate and then he was off.'

'You mean he didn't try . . .'

'He didn't try anything. Didn't so much as try to kiss me.'

She could hear the relief in Doreen's voice. 'Thank goodness for that!' she said. 'If he was set on you, Kim, you wouldn't have stood a chance, believe me, love. I . . .' she broke off. 'Look, I've got to go. Edward is standing here making signs. Now you're sure you won't be seeing him again? You . . .'

'Positive,' said Kimberley. And shortly afterwards she was going upstairs thinking disconsolately that her idea had been a good one—while it lasted.

She undressed, washed, and brushed out her long hair, had her tablet bottle in her hand before she decided against taking one. She didn't want to be soothed into a tranquillised sleep. Far better to stay awake and try and find some other way of keeping Bramcote.

She still hadn't come up with any answer when ten minutes later, the phone went again. It had to be Doreen, she thought, nobody ever rang at this time of night. She reached out a hand for the phone, hoping her good friend hadn't thought up another half dozen questions to bombard her with on the subject of Slade Darville's escort duties.

But when she heard the voice at the other end, not Doreen Gilbert's, but that of Slade Darville himself, she was so shaken she couldn't speak for a while.

'Did I tell you,' he said, his voice, smooth, cool, 'that you were the most beautiful woman at the party?'

'I . . .' Kimberley started to say.

Then realisation was upon her that since he had bothered to get to a phone, bothered to look up her number, then he must have meant it when he had said, 'I'll give you a ring some time.' He might still want to see her! She—she might have a second chance!

'Er—you forgot to mention it,' she said, starting to feel good inside. She just wasn't going to muff that second chance. Bramcote was too important.

She heard a warmth enter his tones. 'Are you free tomorrow evening?' He paused, waiting for her to answer, while Kimberley was thinking things were happening too fast, followed by the thought—but they had to move fast. She had just over five months in which to complete the terms of her father's will . . . 'Or,' Slade was asking, 'do I have to join a long, long queue?'

'Are—are you used to queueing?' she enquired, beset by nerves, knowing she should agree to go out with him, to get this ball rolling.

'No, I'm not,' he admitted. 'Though in your case I'm prepared to make a slight exception.' Kimberley swallowed at the implication behind that, that the attraction of her had lasted more than an hour. Then his voice had toughened. 'But if you can't see me before . . .' he paused again, 'next Wednesday, then we might just as well scrub round it now.'

Kimberley panicked. 'I'll see you tomorrow,' she said quickly.

'We'll have dinner. I'll pick you up . . .'

'We could dine here.' It was out, her thoughts going to his pocket and how if he was an out-of-work actor he wouldn't have money to throw around, before it came to her that she didn't want him in her home. She hadn't dined with anyone except her father since David.

'If you can cook as good as you look, you're on.' Slade Darville had accepted before she could take back her invitation.

'Goodnight,' she said, and put the phone down quickly. She had invented a game she didn't know how to play, and she knew the danger of giving herself away if she stayed talking to him.

Kimberley awakened in the morning with the full realisation of what she was doing upon her. She washed, dressed, and walked lingeringly through every room in the house, and only then knew she was right to be doing what she was. She couldn't give up Bramcote, she thought fiercely, not without a fight. And it wasn't as though she was hurting anybody. Doreen had convinced her that Slade Darville's heart never became involved in any of his amours, convinced her he would rush for a divorce if he ever went so far as to get himself married.

Not that Kimberley was certain she could get him to the point of actually proposing and then marrying her. Her faith in her abilities where men were concerned still rocky from her experience with David, she was having grave doubts on that score. But as she saw it she had two alternatives, both to be played by ear. Either she could try and get him to marry her in a flush of ardour—she crimsoned herself at that thought, wondering in the light of day if she could bear to let any man's mouth rest where David's had lain, but facing that if things went that way she would have to steel herself to accept Slade's kisses. Or, if he looked like cooling, she could offer him some of what her father had left her. Out-of-work actors were notoriously hard up. Perhaps that was the better of the two alternatives. The only snag there was that her father hadn't left her such a lot. Slade might not think it enough to give up his freedom for—even if it was only for long enough for her to get that all-important marriage certificate.

Because there was very little in the house in the way of food, she went into the village during the morning and bought a steak that would have done her for four meals, the humour in the situation catching her unawares, as she found herself thinking, 'The way to a man's heart . . .' She wiped the unaccustomed smile off her face—it wasn't funny. This was deadly serious.

She had been ready for some time when at eight o'clock that night Slade Darville strolled casually up the front garden path. Kimberley swallowed down the agitation in her as she went to the door to let him in. It had been another hot day, and it was still close, which probably accounted for the fact that he was dressed casually in slacks and shirt.

She forced a smile of greeting to her lips, but the smile didn't reach her eyes as he made no move to come forward as she stepped back, but stood, those dark blue eyes going over her face, her sleeveless blouse, and her long cotton skirt.

'Just as I remembered you,' he said, his eyes taking in her hair, dressed exactly as it had been last night.

'Come in,' she said, trying for a light note.

She was uncomfortably aware of him as he followed her into the living room. She had no idea what to say to him, but she knew she was going to have to make an effort if he wasn't to begin to suspect how things really were with her—that she wanted his name, but not his company.

In the living room he handed her a bottle of wine, his contribution to the evening. 'You shouldn't have,' she said straight away, seriously, her thoughts on his impecunious state. The wine was one her father liked and not cheap, she knew.

'It's only a bottle of wine,' he said easily.

'Would you like a drink?' she enquired politely.

'I'm starving,' he said, which threw her, because the next line she had ready was, 'I thought we'd eat in half an hour.'

'We'll eat now, then, shall we?' she offered primly, then saw that since he was an out-of-work actor he probably hadn't eaten at all that day and that was the reason his stomach had overcome good manners.

She took him to the dining room, leaving him there while she hurried to the kitchen. Leaning on the kitchen sink for a moment, she gave herself a repeat of the pep talk she had given herself up in her bedroom earlier when her hand had strayed to her bottle of tranquillisers. She hadn't taken one then, for all she had felt the need. She needed to be fully alaet, needed to try her own hand at acting. It was important, she reminded herself as she turned on the grill. Bramcote was at stake.

'I've poured you a drink.'

She jumped, turned at the unexpected sound of Slade's voice in her kitchen. He came forward and she tried not to get annoyed that he must have opened up the drinks cabinet—virtually empty apart from the couple of bottles she had invested in that day—and found a bottle opener and glasses.

'Thank you,' she said, turning to check the grill.

A glass was pushed into her hand. 'You're uptight,' Slade said coolly by her side. 'Relax, I don't bite.' She looked at him and saw his grin surface. 'Well, not usually,' he added.

After that, strangely, Kimberley did start to unwind. Slade proved himself witty without being grating, and as the first course—another investment in the shape of thawed-out frozen smoked salmon—was followed by steak and salad, and she took another sip of wine, Kimberley warmed to the idea of either getting him to do the proposing or doing the asking herself. There was no rush, though, there were months to go yet.

He wasn't so bad after all, she thought, as he declined her offer of strawberry mousse, settling for cheese and biscuits instead. None of his remarks had been what she would call 'forward', she thought, pleased, something she had rather been dreading. And for any girl who was that way interested, he wasn't so bad looking. His eyes were nicely spaced, his nose straight apart from that small suggestion of a hump on the bridge, and his mouth, which she had thought didn't look to curve too readily, had curved several times when he had looked across at her this evening. It was rather a nice mouth, she thought, then felt nerves begin to bite when she saw he had caught her staring at him.

'Have you had enough to eat?' she asked quickly. 'More cheese?' she offered.

'My hunger for food is satisfied,' he replied, his eyes on her face, making her heart go thump at what was implied by that remark—that he was still hungry, but not for food.

'Shall we—go back to the living room?' Kimberley was on her feet needing to be doing something.

'I'll help you with the washing up,' he suggested.

'No,' she said, more sharply than she meant, not wanting him in the domestic atmosphere of the kitchen. She forced a smile. 'I can do it later.'

He didn't press it, but rose too. 'As you wish,' he said easily.

On the way to the living room, she sought for a new topic that would take his mind from the channel it had taken. She had decided against asking him about his profession since, when he hadn't said one word about any of the plays he had been in, she had gathered from his silence on the subject that he must be sensitive about not having any work at the moment. But she had to get his mind off that other subject—her own mind was rearing away from travelling that route.

Once back in the living room she was ready, insensitive to his feelings or not, to ask him about the only subject that presented itself. But before she could get as far as asking him if Slade Darville was his own name or his stage name, she felt his arm come about her, and then everything within her froze.

'Thank you for my dinner,' he said softly, and was pulling her round to face him before she knew what he was about.

'It—was a pleasure,' she found from somewhere in the icy coldness that had come to her—an icy coldness that blanked out any thought that she stood to lose Bramcote if she didn't make some show of participating.

Slade pulled her close up to him, his head coming nearer. Kimberley stiffened, pushed against his chest in panic, not wanting to feel those lips on hers, those lips that now looked sensuous—she wanted David's lips, not his.

'What's wrong?' Still holding her, those dark blue eyes narrowing, Slade refused to let her back away.

But Kimberley couldn't take it. She wanted him to go. She must have been mad to think she could go through with this, even for Bramcote. She pushed again, struggling to be free, and found to her surprise that Slade wasn't interested in having her in his arms unwillingly.

She took a few hurried steps away and went to stand looking sightlessly out of the window. Tears inside her wanted to empty out, and valiantly she struggled for composure, and conquered her tears, but she was agitated again when she heard Slade come to stand behind her.

'You're trembling,' he said, not touching her, his voice strangely soothing. 'You don't like being rushed, is that it?' he asked, finding excuses for what to him must appear to be the oddest behaviour. No doubt, she thought, most of the women he knew melted once he took them in his arms.

She nodded. 'Y—yes,' she stammered, grasping at the excuse he offered.

'Turn round, Kimberley.'

The soothing note had gone, but his voice was kind. And although she didn't want to turn, there was such a quiet authority in him, plus the fact that he could have touched her again and physically turned her round had he wanted to, that hesitantly she turned.

But she couldn't look at him. She fastened her eyes on his shirt, knowing she had ruined everything. She felt too churned up at that moment to want anything but that he should go.

'Look at me,' he commanded.

Slowly she raised her eyes, deep wide pools of hazel looking back at him. She hoped he wasn't going to start getting aggressive since his plans for how the evening was going to end had been thwarted. She didn't think she could take the aggression that that firm chin on him denoted he had a plentiful supply of.

Slade didn't grow aggressive, but while she stood staring at him fearing the worst, slowly a smile broke from him for her.

'Now,' he said, 'trust me. Trust me and close your eyes.' Solemnly she stared at him without complying. 'Trust me, Kimberley,' he said softly.

Why she closed her eyes then, she didn't know. For she didn't know, even though they had spent over an hour in each other's company, whether he was to be trusted or not. Her eyes closed, she felt something brush against her mouth. And as her eyes flew open, she realised that Slade Darville, without taking hold of her again, had just kissed her.

'You . . .' she began.

'Did that hurt?' he enquired before she could get farther.

Kimberley swallowed hard. It hadn't hurt at all. 'Not too much,' she answered, never having met a man like him before, and unprepared for what he had to say next.

Deliberately he studied her face. Then, his eyes still watching, he asked, 'Is that the first time you've been kissed since your engagement ended?'

Immediately anger she hadn't known in a long time flared, 'Who told you about that?' she snapped, moving a step away, and saw Slade Darville wasn't an atom put out that he had fired her anger to life.

'Edward Gilbert,' he answered easily. 'Though he couldn't tell me who broke the engagement, you or the ex-fiancé.'

Her flare of anger had rapidly cooled, and an iced up feeling came to her again that he could so lightly talk of something that had shattered her world. The ice thickened when Slade stretched his arms forward as if to capture her. 'Ten months is a long time between kisses,' he said. 'Come here, Kimberley.'

She moved in the opposite direction, turning from him. She wanted to be away from him. She had nothing to say to him. Then she found that the sensitivity she had allowed him and his feelings by not bringing up his lack of employment was non-existent when it came to what she wanted to keep hidden. For he showed no sensitivity at all when it came to probing.

'Who did the breaking off?' he pressed, his voice near, telling her he had no objection to following her about the room.

'Does it matter?' she snapped icily, and turned to face him, her chin tilted.

'Not to me,' he replied carelessly, only a yard from her. 'Though if you had moments of trying to freeze him off the way you're trying with me, then I can't say I blame him for taking to his heels.'

Anger sparked to life again at his comment. It hadn't been like that with David, it just hadn't! But this time, before she could give vent to her anger in a short and sharp reply, it came to her in a lightning flash that, knowing she was trying to freeze him by her attitude, Slade Darville was nowhere near to being frozen off. He was still here with her, wasn't he? Did that mean he was still attracted to her? He could be forgiven for leaving when she had pushed him away not long ago, only—he hadn't left!

'D—David,' she said, surmounting the hurdle of bringing out his name to this other man she wanted to marry her, though for vastly different reasons, 'did take to his heels, as you put it.' And explaining because she had to give if she was going to take, 'But not because of anything I did—I don't think.' Her voice faltered. 'He—he just—fell out of love with me,' she said, a knife turning in her, 'and—in love with someone else.' It was out, said. Said to someone who was almost a stranger. And she felt weak from the effort of it. She mastered her emotions. 'I'm sorry I was snappy,' she apologised, and confessed, 'I'm a bit on edge.'

Slade took a step that did away with the space between them. Then, as though he liked having her there, he took her in his arms. 'You were edgy when I arrived,' he said, his hold loose, his face serious as he looked down at her and added, 'With your father dying so recently, it's understandable, Kimberley.' Then quietly, 'It becomes more understandable when taken into account is the fact that it's almost a year since you last entertained an—admirer.'

Not trembling this time to find herself in his arms, Kimberley wanted to get off this subject that would have her near to tears again. And she saw then that there was only one way to do that, much though it went against the grain.

'So you—admire me?'

She saw how well she had succeeded in changing the subject when Slade looked into her face, a fire lighting his eyes.

'If I showed you how much,' he said, a complex man if ever she met one in direct contrast to that fire, and his arms fell away from her, 'I would probably have you backing away again.' Her agitation at his remark was quietened, when he followed it up with,

'As it is—believe it. Now I think it's time I made tracks for my bed.'

It was still early, but Kimberley wasn't sorry he was going. She found him confusing, and didn't like the feeling. She walked along the hall with him.

'You don't live locally, do you?' she enquired, conversation coming to her more easily now he was on the verge of leaving.

'My base is London,' he told her at the door, 'but I'm putting up at the village pub for a while.'

The door was open and soon she would be alone again. 'I've—enjoyed this evening,' she made herself say, and saw from his look that he didn't believe her.

'You'll have a pimple on your tongue in the morning,' he said softly, and before she knew what he was about, he had bent and kissed her, and had gone.

It should have been relief that rushed in when she had closed the door after him, but it wasn't. He was staying in the village, but had made no mention of seeing her again.

Kimberley went into the dining room and began clearing away, wondering if she was any further forward in her quest to get herself a husband.

She was in the kitchen tackling the washing up when one very certain fact made itself known. Slade Darville was going to have to do the proposing. There was something about him, she didn't know quite what, maybe the way he always seemed to say and act in the opposite way from that she was expecting, that had her wary, scared, of asking him to marry her.

Oddly enough she slept well that night. She was out of bed as sun streamed through her bedroom window, and was bathed and dressed and downstairs sipping tea before she realised she had gone to sleep dry-eyed last night.

She was busy with a duster, in the middle of wondering if Slade Darville was up yet; these acting types slept late, she was sure. Or perhaps he was out of his

bed and had already vacated his room at the Rose and
Crown, she was thinking, when the front door bell
went.

'A duster suits you,' said the object of her thoughts.
'But you can dust any old time. Can you come out to
play?'

It was the first of many outings with Slade Darville.
He called every day, always unannounced. The weather was perfect. They walked, talked, picnicked, had
taken a boat out on the river. And though Kimberley
was more often than not guarded with him, there were
occasions, as each day followed, when she was more
natural with him. He always kissed her on parting, but
as if he could sense her withdrawal, his kisses remained
like that fleeting kiss he had given her that first night
he had entered her house.

She admitted to herself that she was learning to be
more comfortable with him. So much so that when last
night, after two weeks of seeing him every day, he had
been about to leave for what he called his 'digs', a
theatre term if ever she heard one, it had been she who
had raised up her face to receive his kiss.

But his kiss hadn't happened straight away. Her vo-
lunteering to be kissed had halted him. He had looked
at her for long moments, and then that smile of his
had come out.

'Goodnight, sweet Kimberley,' he had said, and had
kissed her just as lightly as before.

Kimberley raced round her housework that Sunday
morning, expecting any second to hear his familiar
tattoo on the kitchen door. That he no longer came to
the front door was a mark of how their friendship had
progressed.

At lunch time, when he hadn't arrived, she was beginning to feel disquieted. Where was he? Things had
been going so well. That he did not seem to be the
rake Doreen had said he was, she was sure, because

Slade was respecting that she was still a little off balance from losing her father.

She now had less than five months left to get him to put a gold band on her finger. It was important that not a moment was wasted.

Not feeling like eating lunch, Kimberley took her writing materials into the kitchen. She was still hopeful of seeing him coming up the garden path with that long-legged stride of his, as she got down to answering letters from friends that there had been no time to answer during the past two weeks.

Her letters finished at three, she returned her writing case to where it belonged, and was just returning to the kitchen, when the knock she had spent all morning listening for sounded at the kitchen door.

There was a smile on her face as she opened it. 'Did I tell you you have the prettiest nose I've ever seen?' said Slade.

'Come in,' she said, her face returning to its usual unsmiling look. And airily, since he was so offhand— six hours late—although he hadn't said he would call at all. 'You've only just caught me. I was just off out to post some letters.'

'Are they important?'

'They've waited a fortnight.'

He grinned, knowing he was the culprit. 'Come and have a farewell picnic with me,' he said. And while she looked at him incredulously—he couldn't go yet, he couldn't, not before he had married her!—he added, 'I have to return to London tomorrow.'

CHAPTER THREE

SHE should have been more forthcoming, Kimberley saw as she crossed fields and meadows with Slade, him carrying the plastic carrier with the picnic food he must have got them to prepare at the Rose and Crown. She should have brought up the subject of his work. For it was clear now that he must have been in regular contact with his London agent and had a part he was to start rehearsing tomorrow.

The idea of her doing the proposing came to her again as silently she trudged beside him. But what was the good of putting the proposition to him now? Before, when he hadn't any work, he might have considered it. But what chance had she now that he would take the meagre sum she could offer him when he had work and money from his own efforts coming in?

They came to a brook, Slade took her hand to help her across the stepping stones—and she was back with David, remembering how David had helped her across at this same spot. How it was David who had come to grief by slipping off the stone, and had stood in six inches of water, not at all amused that she had burst out laughing.

'No sad thoughts today.'

Kimberley looked up, about to reach the bank. Slade was looking at her as though he could read her mind, knew her thoughts had been far away with her ex-fiancé. She didn't want Slade Darville intruding on her private thoughts. Her unfriendly gaze went from him, to see the sun had gone in.

'It's clouded over,' she said. She wanted to go back. What was the use of going on? She would never get Slade to propose in the short time she had left. She might as well throw the towel in here and now.

'It's still hot,' he said, giving her hand a tug, so she had to finish crossing the brook.

She was glad he was in a quiet mood too as they settled down to eat their picnic. What he was thinking about that he offered very little in the way of conversation, she didn't know, and didn't particularly want to. All she saw was that she had spent two weeks of seeing him every day. Had gone against her natural inclination not to go anywhere with him—though to be fair those outings had never been boring; Slade's mind was much too alert for it ever to be dull when he was around. But what outcome did she have? For all her plottings and plannings, she was still going to lose Bramcote.

'Shall we go back?' she suggested as soon as they had finished off chicken legs, tomatoes and sandwiches, and the remains were all stuffed back in the plastic carrier.

'Don't be in such a rush,' Slade said easily, reminding her when she didn't need to be reminded. 'I shall be back in the hurly-burly of London tomorrow. I want to enjoy the peace and tranquility here on my last day.'

Disgruntled, Kimberley lay down and closed her eyes. Let him get on with his peace and tranquility! she thought, put out, stifling a sigh as she wondered if she would ever know peace and tranquility again.

'Do you always wear your hair in that style?'

Get on with your peace and tranquility and leave me alone, she wanted to say. 'What's wrong with it?' she asked grumpily—and was further peeved when he burst out laughing.

She opened her eyes and felt a mixture of emotions start up inside that Slade wasn't sitting staring out at the view from their hilltop vantage point, but was lying close to her propped up on one elbow, and was looking nowhere but at her. He's too close, she thought, wanting to get up and run.

'You've got them on you today, haven't you?' he remarked pleasantly. 'Now what can I do to sweeten you up?'

His head came nearer. He had kissed her before. She had grown accustomed to the fleeting meeting of mouths. He looked deeply into her eyes, then she saw nothing as his lips touched hers and moved away again.

'I was going to say,' he said with a teasing smile, 'that I see nothing wrong with the way you wear your hair.' He kissed her lightly again. 'It shows up your tiny delicate ears.'

Kimberley sensed he wasn't as teasing as he was making out when the tiny delicate ears he had referred to were next to be saluted by his lips. She went to sit up, but found Slade's hand on her shoulder keeping her down.

A feeling akin to panic tried to get started, making her want to push at him to let her free, but his head came down again as he moved off his elbow and leaned over her.

She didn't want him to kiss her—not like this. Her heart was beating wildly as his kiss deepened. She closed her eyes thinking of all the things she should have done to keep Bramcote, but hadn't. Was there still time?

Shaking inside, she made herself put her arms around him, and had to grip tightly when, as he felt what he must have thought was her response, Slade plundered her mouth, then went from there to draw her dress from her throat so his lips could take pleasure there.

She gripped him again when his mouth claimed hers once more, her nails digging in for control as one hand slowly caressed its way to her breast. David! her mind cried, wanting to hit Slade's hand way from her as she turned her face away so he shouldn't see she was choking with a mixture of emotions at what seemed a betrayal of her love for David.

His hand left her breast, and the sound of his voice brought her out of conflict. 'Don't you ever kiss back?' he asked gruffly.

'I . . .' she faltered, 'it's—been a long time.'

She saw impatience in him at her answer. 'Then you have a lot of wasted time to make up for,' he said aggressively, and his mouth had captured hers again, leaving her in no doubt that he wanted her. His hands caressed her body, and conflict was in her again.

That was until she felt his hand come under the skirt of her dress, felt him begin to caress her thigh, and then conflict flew as instinct alone had her pushing at him. She had sprung to her feet, her breath coming in short gasps as she fought for control.

'Don't—don't do that,' she said shakily, her back to him. He too was on his feet.

Slade turned her so he could see into her pale face. For long unsmiling minutes they faced each other, Slade keeping hold of her, a hand on each shoulder. Tension was in the air, was all around, made even more tense when at last he said:

'Marriage or nothing?'

The heavens opened. Thunder rattled. But Slade didn't let go of her. And as rain battered at them, Kimberley made no movement, but just stood and stared back at him.

Her hands clenched, her heart thudding, there was a constriction in her throat. Then, 'Yes,' she said solemnly, 'marriage or nothing.'

Slade held her eyes for three long agonising seconds, as Kimberley waited. Then his glance went to the rising and falling front of her rain-sodden dress.

'We'd better make a run for it,' he said.

He was bossy when they reached the house, and she didn't like it. Anticlimax, a damp squib, had her sharp with him when he told her to go upstairs, to take a hot bath and change her things.

Mutinously she glared at him. 'I'll do it when you've gone,' she said, fed up with him, with everything.

'I'll still be here when you come down,' he told her, with cool cheek, since she hadn't invited him to stay. And jibing, 'What's the matter? Afraid to be naked with me around?'

Colour flared at his comment. It hadn't entered her head that he might pursue the intimacies begun up on that hill once they were back in the house.

'You wouldn't . . .'

'Oh, for God's sake,' he muttered. 'Get going before I start thinking of doing just that.'

Kimberley went, locking herself in the bathroom as a precaution, even though from his last remark it was obvious that no such idea of invading her privacy had entered his head.

She rubbed her hair as dry as she could make it, but it was still damp when with the expertness of usage she quickly flipped it into a knot at the back of her head. She felt calmer when, dressed in shirt and jeans, she went back to the kitchen where she had left Slade.

He had dry trousers on when she went in and was just lifting his shirt out of the tumble-drier he must have fathomed out how to use.

His chest was broad and muscular. Kimberley averted her eyes as he shrugged into his shirt and buttoned it—though she suspected his eyes had never left her, for when she looked at him again, his eyes were still on her. Unspeakingly, she stood by the door.

'Come here, Kimberley,' he commanded, his tone cool, but with such note of authority that even while objecting to it, she found her feet moving towards him.

She stopped when she was two yards away—a safe distance, she thought, if he was going to make a grab for her. But Slade didn't make a grab for her. His eyes still stayed with her, but his attitude became casual as he then pushed his hands into his trouser pockets.

'So,' he said, looking at her consideringly, 'it has to be marriage, does it?'

Kimberley's heart set up a riot that he had not forgotten the subject she had thought, up there on the hill, he had no time for.

'Yes,' she said, striving to sound as cool as he, but her voice choked, barely audible.

A drawn-out pause followed, where Slade continued to look at her in that speculative way. Then, his voice as casual as his attitude, he asked, 'Is it all right with you if I make the necessary arrangements?'

It was Saturday. Kimberley awoke and lay there making no attempt to get up. The weather had turned fine again after that cloudburst last Sunday. Happy the bride that the sun shines on, she thought dully, and sat up, ousting thoughts that it should be David she should be marrying today, not Slade Darville.

She made her mind stay with Slade. She hadn't seen him since Sunday, though he had telephoned to say all the arrangements had been made and that he would pick her up for them to go to the register office this morning.

His proposal with the rain bucketing down outside could in no way be compared to David's proposal that sunny day out there in the orchard. David's proposal had been so romantic, his 'Darling, I love you desperately, please say you'll marry me' just wasn't in the same field as the proposal Slade had uttered.

She forced David out of her mind again as she recalled how she hadn't been sure at first that Slade's 'Is it all right with you if I make the necessary arrangements?' had been a proposal at all.

She had looked at him, thrown into confusion at the direct way he was looking at her, teetering on the brink of excitement that her chance to keep Bramcote might still be within her grasp.

'Well,' he had questioned, nothing lover-like about him, 'do I arrange for you to become Mrs Slade Darville at the first opportunity or not?'

So it was a proposal! Kimberley checked on the ela- tion that would have her rapidly agreeing to say yes. Ought she to tell him that she didn't love him—could never love anybody again? She recalled then all the things Doreen had said about him, realised too that all this proposal was about was that Slade knew he couldn't get her any other way. He didn't want a mar- riage that would last either. Why mess it up with bringing talk of love into it? Slade didn't love her, she could be certain of that. There had been no word of love in his proposal.

Her lips dry, she had moistened them. 'Yes,' she said, having no objection to raise to his 'at the first opportunity' either, since the sooner she had that mar- riage certificate, the sooner Bramcote would be ensured as hers.

Slade's face had taken on a shuttered look at her confirmation that she would marry him, so she couldn't tell how he had taken her acceptance. But when he moved as though to come towards her, she had moved out of range—she had thrown herself at David when he had proposed, but Slade wasn't David.

'I'd prefer a register office ceremony,' had come blurting from her.

Slade halted. 'Sounds as though you've given the matter some thought,' he drawled.

He would never know how much. 'It was only last month that my father died,' she said quietly, guilt smiting her that she was bringing him into this, even though if he hadn't made his will the way he had, she wouldn't have needed his help this way.

'So you'd like to keep it quiet.'

The fewer people who knew about it the better as far as she was concerned. Thank goodness Doreen was away. With luck she could be married to Slade and divorced from him before she came back, and no one in the village any the wiser.

Slade had then got down to the business of jotting down the details he thought he would need, saying he would call in at the register office in Thaxly on his way to London tomorrow morning, and that she was to leave everything to him.

He had kissed her in parting and she hadn't backed away, knowing, since he had said he would be too busy in London to see her before Saturday, that she mustn't endanger that wedding coming off on Saturday by showing him in these last few minutes that she didn't want his kisses.

The thought of Slade's kisses had Kimberley hurrying from her bed. She didn't dare let herself think about what was to happen that night, when Slade was under her roof. The only way this whole thing could be got through was for her to take it a step at a time. Once she was married to him, everything else would have to sort itself out. Though she was praying as hard as she could that Slade wouldn't raise too many objections when he discovered she had manoeuvred a single bed into the dressing room that adjoined hers. Common sense told her she had no chance of denying him her body—it was what he was marrying her for, wasn't it? But she wasn't going to have him in her bed all night if she could help it. all night if she could help it.

The ringing of the phone, an unexpected call from Dr Ellis, was a welcome relief from her thoughts. 'How are you, Kimberley?' he asked. 'I would have been to see you, but I've been rushed off my feet.'

'I feel fine,' she replied. But she wasn't sorry he was too busy to stay chatting—though she couldn't help thinking how very fortunate the Amberton people were to have such a caring man to look after them. Not many doctors, rushed as he was, would take time out to ring patients they liked to keep an eye on.

She frowned at the thought that Dr Ellis was still

keeping an eye on her. Then she mused that perhaps it was usual in view of her recent bereavement. Though she was glad he couldn't see the state she was in when later she went to get ready for her marriage. Dr Ellis would have discounted the 'I feel fine' she had given him after only half a look at her.

Her hands were shaking so much she had difficulty in securing the tiny buttons down the front of the cream-coloured two-piece. The two-piece was unworn, bought because David had liked it. Kimberley pushed memory of him away. She was in this too deep now to start thinking of David, to start having second thoughts on what she was about to do.

She was ready and with time to spare, time hanging heavily on her hands, for she couldn't very well look for something to do since she stood the risk of getting a mark on her cream silk if she pottered about. Besides, because she had needed to keep busy this week, there wasn't a room in the house that hadn't been turned out.

The sound of the front door bell made her jump, and she looked at the clock. Slade would be here in five minutes. She wondered about slipping on an overall to hide her wedding finery, not wanting anyone from the village to see she was dressed up obviously for something out of the ordinary.

The bell went again, forcing her to abandon the idea. She wanted to get rid of whoever it was before Slade arrived. She went along the hall and pulled back the door. Slade had already arrived.

'I expected you to come round the back!' Kimberley exclaimed, surprise at seeing him in a suit for the first time, an expensively cut suit at that, making the exclamation leave her without thought.

'Today is special, wouldn't you say?' he asked, and was over the threshold and had taken her in his arms before she could think up a reply to that.

He kissed her long and lingeringly. Kimberley put

her hands on his shoulders, but more to steady herself than in supplication.

'You're trembling,' he observed, letting go of her, 'Nervous?'

She nodded. Nervous was an understatement. Yet nothing would have her going back from what she had chosen to do. 'Do you want a coffee or anything before we leave?' she enquired.

'I want to marry you,' Slade said seriously, and walked to the living room with her.

'N-no trouble in getting the day off?' she asked, wondering if he was skipping a rehearsal as she picked up her bag and gloves.

'I've brought some work with me,' he replied, and smiled as he looked at her and added, 'though I don't think it will get done.'

She didn't think too much of his reply, but didn't think this was the moment to tell him she wouldn't mind at all if he spent the whole of the weekend studying the lines of his play.

Having not thought about how they were going to get to Thaxly, but hoping, since the way she was dressed might draw attention if they went by bus, that he had thought to hire a taxi, Kimberley saw with some surprise that Slade had arrived in a very plush type of car which would certainly raise comment if it was seen in the village.

She got inside without comment, the thought passing through her mind that he had hired it for the occasion, and she hoped he wouldn't be too much out of pocket as a consequence.

Slade didn't start the car straight away, but reached on to the back seat and pulled forward a most lovely spray of freesias—and, having come equipped, extracted a pin from behind his lapel.

'Do you mind a pinhole in your suit?' he asked, as the heady perfume assailed her, and as she shook her head, he attached them to her jacket with deft fingers.

'Now you really do look as if you're going to be married,' he said.

Kimberley did not feel married after the ceremony. She had a gold ring on the third finger of her left hand, but the ceremony had left her unmoved, save that when Slade had uttered his responses in a firm voice she had felt the pull of tears that he wasn't David.

But she was grateful to Slade for having married her, even though he had his own reasons for doing so, and elation came to her as they stepped into the street outside, her eyes shining, though not with unshed tears. She had done it! Bramcote was hers.

'Happy?' Slade asked quietly, not missing her shining eyes.

Ecstatic wouldn't have been an understatement, she thought then. 'Sublimely,' she murmured. And, in her intense gratitude to him, there in the High Street, she stood on tiptoe and kissed him. She drew back too late to realise what she had done.

'I had booked a table at the Swan for lunch,' said Slade, gripping her arm tightly. 'But if you'd rather go home . . .'

He left the rest of his sentence unsaid. He didn't need to finish it as sanity returned to Kimberley and she realised just what she had triggered off.

'I'm starving,' she said, as he had once, her elation scattering.

It returned when he laughed at her reply. 'For food, I gather, from the expression on your face!'

Kimberley was happy at that meal, and it showed. She had never been overly talkative with Slade, but at that wedding lunch she chatted and laughed, entirely unaware that the girl she had been twelve months ago was coming to life, and that the man she had just married had nothing but admiration in his eyes.

His eyes too were alight when the last drop of coffee was drunk and he took hold of her hand across the table.

'Ready to go home now, Kim?' he enquired softly.

'I . . .' Vivacity fell away. Her sudden trembling communicated itself to him, so that his eyes narrowed.

He let go her hand, signalling to the waiter for the bill. Then he turned back to her, his voice easy. 'No rush,' he said casually, just his tone enough to calm her. 'Fancy going to the cinema?'

Kimberley looked down at the corsage of fragrant freesias he had given her, her cream silk suit, and had to laugh. 'You're joking!' she protested.

'You're getting to know me,' he said, and laughed too before suggesting, 'Why don't we go back to Bramcote, change out of our glad rags and . . .' he saw she had tensed, 'and go for a walk?'

'It—sounds like a good idea to me,' she said. She was smiling as they left the Swan. She was going home to Bramcote, and it was all hers.

It was when they reached Bramcote that the joy within her took a dip. She stood with Slade, about to lead the way in, then watched when he walked from her and to the boot of the car. The suitcase he extracted was sizeable, causing her to bite her lip on the thought that sped in—how long was he staying? How long before he got tired of her?

They walked into the house together. 'Going to show me where I can deposit this?' Slade asked, when in the hall she hesitated, wondering if she could delay the moment by making a cup of tea or something.

'Of course,' she said, and went to the foot of the stairs, her insides churning that she hadn't had the nerve to prepare a room for him as far distant from her own as possible.

She opened the door of her bedroom, looked quickly away from him as she saw his eyes take in the faded wallpaper, her double bed.

'There's a bathroom here,' she said in a rush, indicating another door in the room, not surprised to see

her hand was shaking. It was the way she felt all over.
'And,' she went forward to the dressing room door,
searching for every ounce of tact, 'I—er—thought,
since I'm—er—such a very restless sleeper, you might
prefer—to—er—sleep in here.' Not daring to look at
him—his silence was ominous, she thought, trying not
to get panicky—she gabbled on. 'My wardrobes are
full—th-they're empty in there.'

She stood aside as, without a word, Slade brushed
past her, slinging his case inside. Still without a word
he shrugged out of his jacket. When his tie came off
and he began to unbutton his shirt, Kimberley moved.

He had said something about a walk, about changing
before they went out, she recalled, hanging on to that
thought as she scooped up jeans and a shirt and shut
herself away in the bathroom. She made no attempt to
change as she tried to come to terms with the fact that,
much as she wanted her marriage to end right here,
she owed something to Slade, and had a very clear
feeling that he was just not the sort of man to let her
get away with less than what he had temporarily given
up his freedom for.

She took several deep steadying breaths, then started
to get out of her wedding finery. She caught a glimpse
of her tense looking face in a mirror, and avoided looking in the mirror again.

She thought she had mastered the panic that had
threatened to consume her when she had bolted into
the bathroom. But one look at the set expression on
Slade's face when she emerged and found him in her
bedroom was enough to have her insides acting up
again.

'I think,' he said, his eyes steady on hers, 'that it's
about time I evened up accounts.'

'Evened up accounts?' she queried, her voice husky;
she had no idea what he meant, but she was wary of
him.

He moved, came forward, not once taking his eyes

from her face. 'You're one kiss up on me since our marriage,' he said quietly, and the next thing she knew, he had reached for her, and she was in his arms.

His head came nearer, and she just knew he had forgotten all about his suggestion that they should take a walk. 'Not yet,' shot from her before his mouth could touch hers. Wild emotions were raging in her. This was all wrong. It should be David, not him.

She saw Slade didn't like her refusing even to kiss him. But his tone was even, still that same quiet voice, as he told her:

'I'm not suggesting bed, so you can stop trembling. I received the message you're transmitting some time ago.' She wasn't sure she dared relax, dared believe what he was saying. And then he smiled. 'But you can't blame me, dear wife, for wanting a short skirmish on the outskirts of our marriage consummation.'

With that his head came forward, and gently his lips claimed hers.

Perhaps she did begin to relax, did believe him when he had said this wasn't the time when he would take her. His words, plus the fact that guilt was prodding her that she wasn't playing fair, now Bramcote was hers, when Slade broke his kiss and looked at her, still holding her in his arms, made Kimberley smile.

'I think I'm a bit screwed up,' she confessed, then put her hands on his shoulders so he should know she was doing her best to play by the rules.

His answer was to kiss her again, his kiss warmer this time. Kimberley ignored the flutter of panic, remembered the talking to she had given herself in the bathroom. He wasn't David, never would be. No one could take David's place. But she owed Slade.

She kissed him back—and to her surprise found it more pleasurable to be a participator than she had thought. Her arms moved round his broad shoulders and his kiss deepened. He groaned softly and drew back, and Kimberley smiled. Everything was going to be all right, she knew it was.

His eyes appeared so dark as to be navy the moment before he kissed her again. She felt his hands at the back of her, gently caressing, then felt them move to her hips—and was disquieted. When he pulled her forward, pressing her against his lean hardness, the illusion that everything was going to be all right promptly faded.

'No,' she said, and was pushing at him.

Slade let her go, his jaw square, an aggressive look to him. She thought she was in for a few not so pleasant words, then discovered she was still nowhere near to knowing anything about the man she had married.

'Let's walk,' he said brusquely.

They had walked, with Kimberley giving herself another pep talk. She had cooked dinner, deciding that nothing else mattered now that she was secure in the knowledge that she didn't have to leave her home.

But as darkness fell she began to get edgy again—half of her wanting her marriage consummated, to have it all over and done with, the other half of her finding it shameful that she could think to betray the love she felt for David in such a manner.

Slade had not attempted to kiss her since that heated few minutes up in her room, though he had put an arm about her as though he was about to while they had been washing up after their meal. But she had jumped, the arm around her was unexpected, and his kiss had never happened as silently he had picked up another plate and begun to dry it.

It was half past ten when the tape they were listening to came to an end. 'I'm going to have a bath,' Kimberley said into the stillness.

'I'll join you presently,' said Slade, and at what she saw as a threat in his words, it was all she could do to force a smile as he stood up and she hurriedly left the room.

She had come to terms with herself again by the

time her bath was over. She had Bramcote, she owed him, she repeated over and over again.

But there was pain in her heart when, keeping the thought that she was in his debt to the front of her, she took one of her nightdresses that had been part of her trousseau and slipped it over her head. Unable to look at the traitor to love she felt herself to be, Kimberley stood away from the mirror as she brushed out her hair.

She heard footsteps coming along the landing and made a dive for the bed; hurriedly pulling the covers round her, realising she had spent an over-long period in her bath.

Slade had to come through her bedroom to reach the small dressing room, and she tried to raise a smile as the door opened and she saw him standing there.

'I haven't used all the hot water,' she said off the top of her head.

Slade closed the door and approached the bed, his eyes feasting on her glorious silky hair, seeing it down for the first time. 'Your hair is beautiful,' he murmured, his voice sounding as if he couldn't wait to bury himself in it.

Then while she was thinking that all thoughts of anything save joining her in her bed were lost to him, Slade stood up and asked if the shower was in working order.

Trying to switch her mind as quickly as he could switch his, she realised that to an outsider the shower unit might look a bit rickety.

'It takes some time to warm up, but yes, it works,' she said.

'Since I'm in no mood to take a cold shower,' he smiled, 'will you promise to stay just as you are until I get back?'

Kimberley heard the water running, then heard it stop. She switched on the bedside lamp and was wondering about switching off the centre light, when Slade came from the bathroom. His eyes stayed on her as, moving to the wall switch, he did the job for her.

He appeared to be wearing only a towelling robe, she saw, and her heart pounded madly as in the glow from the small lamp he came and sat on the edge of her bed.

'You look too ethereal to be touched,' he said softly, and Kimberley knew she looked as pale as she felt when seconds ticked away with Slade just sitting there his eyes taking in her every feature. And then, unhurriedly, he had picked up her trembling hand and was raising it to his lips.

Whether or not the feel of her skin set flame to his chemistry for her, she was too agitated to wonder. But suddenly he had turned her hand over, was planting burning kisses on the inside of her wrist, was kissing her arm. And it was then, with a firm but gentle tug, that he had pulled her until she was in his arms, the smell of his aftershave filling her nostrils as he breathed the possessive words:

'Kimberley—my wife!'

Her covering was flimsy. His hands burning into her flesh as his mouth met hers and his hands caressed her naked shoulders.

She tried hard to participate as she had done before, but this time she didn't have the security of knowing that then they had only been skirmishing on the edge of consummation. This time Slade meant business.

And something froze inside her, not giving her a chance to experience again the pleasure she had found in his kisses earlier.

Slade continued to kiss her, his hands caressing while she just hung on, his hands moving to her breasts, sliding the frail chiffon strap from her shoulder and down her arm when her thin covering prevented him from feeling her nakedness.

She felt his hand warm on her breast and wanted to fight him off; she didn't want his hand there.

Try to imagine it's David, she found herself thinking—and as that thought penetrated, so too did nausea. Nausea at herself, at the obscenity of her thought, disgust that her honesty before her father's death had been unquestionable. Yet here she was married to Slade and on the way to pretending he was another man, the man she loved.

'*No!*' came screaming from her, her face ashen as she pushed at him, scrabbling to the other side of the bed where she could escape him.

She was off the bed, uncaring that Slade didn't look very lover-like now as he overcame the upset to his plans. Unheeding that he didn't look very pleased at this turn of events, with a distraught hand she pushed her hair back from her face. How could she betray the love she had for David, betray her own standards?

'I—can't,' she croaked.

'Can't?' he questioned, a dark look on his face.

'I—I . . .' Hopelessly Kimberley shook her head. 'I can't,' she repeated, her voice a thin thread of sound as her hands came out as though to ward him off, for all he had not moved.

But she knew she was right to fear him when he stood and came slowly towards her, hard aggression rearing.

'You've left it a bit late to discover you *can't*, haven't you?'

'I'm sorry—sorry,' she stammered, her eyes imploring him to understand. 'I—I know that's the only reason you married me—b-because I—wouldn't before.' She saw his brow move at that, and went on to plead, 'B-but I can't!'

He had been gentle with her before, but she only then saw just how gentle he had been. For there was nothing but a terrifying hard aggression in him now as he stretched forward and yanked her into his arms.

'Didn't anyone ever tell you, lovely wife,' he muttered through his teeth, his arms iron bands around her, 'that there's no such word as *can't*?'

And with that his mouth was on hers, cruel as her teeth ground against her mouth, his hands biting where before they had gently soothed. And Kimberley was fighting. The other way, had Slade remained gentle, who knew, he might have coaxed her into submission— she had found his kisses acceptable before. But this way, his mouth making ravaging sorties on her throat, her breasts, there was no chance of her sense of fairness having a hearing, of her giving in.

'No!' she screamed wildly, pushing frantically at him, to no avail.

'No!' he mocked. 'That word isn't in my dictionary either.'

His mouth captured hers as she struggled to be free. She heard the chiffon of her nightdress tear, and was out of his arms as the sound hit him too and his hold slackened.

Her shoulder strap had parted company with the rest of the garment, she saw, as backing around the room she saw his hot gaze on her uncovered breast. Hastily she covered herself up, expecting him to pounce, then saw he was in no hurry, his view from where he was standing being quite satisfactory.

The word, 'No!' left her again, this time in despair.

'No!' Slade taunted. 'You should have thought about this side of marriage, dear wife. But you didn't, did you? Your greedy little mind took over, didn't it, blocking out your aversion to be in anyone's arms but the man's who jilted you.'

Slade Darville knew how to hit, and hit hard. He was right in saying David had jilted her, as grievously as it rocked her to hear him say it. He was right too that she had blocked out her aversion to being in anyone's arms but his. But her panic-stricken mind could make no sense of his accusing her of being greedy. Not unless—unless he had somehow found out about Bramcote!

'It wasn't greed,' she contradicted hurriedly, when he took a step nearer. 'The house is mine by right.'

'House?' Her words had halted him. 'What the hell are you talking about?'

She had stopped him in his tracks, she could see that. 'You know,' she choked. 'Somehow you know.'

'Know what?'

'Why I married you.'

For a moment she thought Slade was going to question her further, then as his eyes once again roamed her body, the chiffon doing little to hide her contours, she realised he thought she was just dangling a red herring to prevent him from taking what he had given up his freedom for—if only for a very short while.

He moved again, and she backed, came up against the wardrobe—and had nowhere else to go as with another stride he had hold of her arms.

'I certainly do know why you married me, my beautiful money-grabbing wife,' he grated. Her eyes widened as his head bent and his lips burned on her naked shoulder. 'You tried to give me the brush-off when I introduced myself at the Gilbert's party. But your attitude underwent a miraculous change, didn't it, after Doreen had given you the lowdown on the state of my wealth.'

His mouth was trailing kisses between the valley of her breasts, when her surprised wavery exclamation of, 'Wealth?' brought his head up.

'Are you going to deny that it didn't occur to you when you finished the discussion I saw you having with Doreen, your eyes in my direction all the time, that you didn't think you'd have a crack at killing two birds with the one stone?'

Nowhere near to understanding what he was talking about, his hands bruising her arms as he made sure she didn't escape him a second time, Kimberley just stood and stared.

'Such a picture of wide-eyed innocence,' he sneered.

'It never crossed your mind, did it, to have yourself a rich husband?'

'Rich husband?' He was as good as broke, she knew he was.

'You're going to say you had no idea?' he mocked. 'That you never for an instant thought to get your own back on all men by withholding from me your—marriage favours?'

'No, no,' she protested, still not believing he was as wealthy as he was intimating. And, shaking her head, 'Doreen didn't tell me anything about you except—except that you have no use for a permanent—relationship.'

He wasn't believing her, she could see that, though he did not deny that he preferred only temporary relationships. 'She didn't tell you either, that apart from money I inherited, I head a not unsuccessful stock-broking business?' he enquired sarcastically.

'No,' she said straight away.

And as she recalled the elegant car he had driven that day, she was aghast as the thought hurtled in that she had pegged him wrong at that party. If he wasn't one of Doreen's waifs and strays then—then he had to be a friend of Edward, Doreen's banker husband!

But even while that incredible thought was sinking in, she was trying to convince him. 'I didn't know, honestly,' she said—and had to suffer his cynical look that he wasn't believing she could be honest about anything. 'You s-said—when I mentioned your work—that you were resting. I thought you were an out-of-work actor.'

'Actor? My God, I must be better at it than I thought,' he said obscurely. Then before she knew what to make of that, his arms were encircling her and she knew he had had enough of talking; action was what he was after. 'I didn't plan to spend this night in verbal discussion,' he said, putting an end to it. 'We'll have plenty of time to talk this out in the morning.'

His ardour had cooled during their conversation, she thought. But that inflamed look of desire was there in his eyes again as he drew her finely clad body up against him.

A violent shaking began inside Kimberley when she felt the heat of him as his hard body pressed her against the wardrobe. The uncontrollable shaking was too wild not to be felt by him, she knew, as tears welled to her eyes and he pulled back so he could look at her. She could protest from now until Doomsday and he would still be set on his course, she thought, as, unable to keep still, speechlessly, she looked back at him with luminous large eyes.

A tear spilled over and rolled down her cheek. Silently a tear fell from her other eye. She knew from the look of him that Slade would be blind to her tears as he had been deaf to her protests. A paroxysm of shuddering took her as his head neared, his mouth half way to possessing hers.

Apart from the shaking that wouldn't leave her, Kimberley stayed still, no longer trying to escape when his cry of, 'Oh God!' left him.

Her feet felt nailed to the floor as his arms fell away. She couldn't have moved then if she had tried. She was past caring that her breast was again exposed to his view when Slade stood back, and was unable to move for an age when, tearing his eyes from her, he growled:

'Hide yourself in bed before I lose my mind!'

CHAPTER FOUR

KIMBERLEY awoke with a sense of foreboding. The memory of how Slade had let her off last night was with her as she opened her eyes. She realised as she came awake to the day that, knowing the reason he had for marrying her at all, she couldn't hope that a second night would pass that would have him leaving her, their marriage still not consummated. And yet it must be as clear to him as last night it had been clear to her that she just couldn't.

A movement by her dressing table had her glance shooting to the man who stood leaning against it idly watching her. She sat up, taking the bedclothes with her, her mouth dry that maybe he wasn't going to wait until evening. That maybe he considered himself cheated.

Slade moved away from the dressing table, his eyes glinting dangerously as he read the alarm in her eyes. 'Take that look off your face,' he told her sharply. 'I'm not in the mood for a repeat performance of scene one.'

Kimberley took a steadying breath. And that was about all she had time for before Slade had come and sat on the edge of her bed. She wanted to get up, she felt stifled with him there. She wished he would go away. But Slade Darville, she saw, was not going anywhere until he had the answer to the question he had to put.

'What are these?' he demanded to know, opening his hand to reveal the bottle of tablets that Kimberley in her agitation of last night had forgotten to return to her dressing table drawer.

She had seen aggression in him before, saw he was

66

in no mood to play games, and the 'It's none of your business' she wanted to fling at him stayed down. She felt too vulnerable with him entitled to share the privacy of her bedroom.

'They're—just tablets the doctor prescribed,' she answered woodenly, and saw his jaw jut that that wasn't any kind of an answer.

'For?' he asked tersely.

Why should she tell him? she thought, beginning to get annoyed. Then she saw from his face that she was likely to have him sitting on her bed all day, or worse, if she didn't.

'If you must know——' she began, then stopped. She didn't want him knowing of her weaknesses, didn't want him to know she was so sensitive sometimes she had difficulty in coping.

'I'm going to know,' Slade stated bluntly, completely unmoved at the shadows that crossed her face.

Kimberley was over the moment of remembering David, of wanting to weep. Slade's blunt aggression had stiffened her.

'I took—my broken engagement—badly,' she said flatly. 'Dr Ellis thought . . .'

'Tranquillisers!' he said, then was snapping abruptly, his voice accusing, 'You've been filling yourself up with this sort of junk since then?'

'He thought I was heading for a nervous breakdown,' she said defensively, looking past him, not seeing why she should have to put up with his castigation, but powerless—unless she wanted to try for the isolation of the bathroom with small chance of getting there without him following her—to do anything else.

A brooding silence hung in the air, Slade considering what she had told him, and Kimberley wishing he would go back to London and stay there.

But his voice had changed when next he spoke. The underlying aggression was still there, but his voice was quietly thoughtful.

'How many do you take a day?'

'I haven't taken any for ages,' she told him. 'I just—just like to keep them handy in case . . .'

'You took one last night?' Aggression was back.

'Yes.' It was her turn to snap.

'Before or after I went to bed?'

Kimberley threw him a look of mutinous dislike. He was aloof to it, waiting, his own look relentless. 'When you left,' she muttered.

'I upset you that much?'

Didn't he know he had? Why did he have to put her through this third degree? Good grief, once he'd taken what he had married her for, he'd be away without giving her another thought!

'Well?' he pressed impatiently.

'Yes,' she said moodily, her eyes flying to his at his insensitivity, when he answered:

'Good.'

'Good?' she exclaimed, wondering what sort of a villain she had married, that he could be so uncaring that she had felt near trauma after the dressing room door had firmly closed.

He stood up, his look hostile. 'It's about time somebody woke you up.'

Annoyance with him flickered to anger. The cruel swine! she thought, fire touching her eyes when he looked mockingly down at her. She moved, intensely irritated by him, saw her movement had drawn his gaze to her naked shoulder peeping out from under the sheet, and paled.

'Get dressed and come downstairs before I remember that as your husband I have certain rights,' he told her roughly.

She glared at his departing, bossy back. He wasn't going to be her husband for very much longer, she fumed as she banged about in the bathroom, entirely unaware that this was the first day in a long time that she had been stirred to seething anger.

She was still wearing her metaphorical 'I hate Slade Darville' hat when, fifteen minutes later, dressed in cool cream linen slacks and a pale green shirt, she went downstairs.

It didn't help matters as she went along the hall kitchenwards, to pass her father's study door, open when it had been closed since his death, to see the man who had started a healthy hate growing in her comfortably ensconced in her father's chair.

'Come in here,' he invited, for all the world as though the study was his, Bramcote his.

Kimberley went in. She wanted to tell him to get out of her father's chair, to leave the study, to get out of her house. But she didn't get the chance.

'So, Mrs Darville,' he said insolently, stoking up fires of anger in her by the careless wave of his hand that indicated she should take the only other chair in the room. 'So why did you marry me?'

Kimberley refused to sit, just as she refused to answer. Slade could go hang before she told him anything!

'Tell me,' he said, his eyes hard as he rephrased his question, 'what it is about me that's so special—that is if I'm supposed to believe you and it wasn't just my money that drew your avaricious little gaze?'

That stung. 'It didn't have to be you,' flew from her. And having said that much she didn't see why she shouldn't do some stinging of her own. 'Any man would have done!'

She then found that when it came to hitting below the belt, Slade Darville outclassed her. His jaw moved, then he was hitting her with:

'Too bad the only man you wanted didn't want you, wasn't it?'

Shock at his brutish remark had tears shimmering, her temper gone. Slade looked away from the pain in her eyes, and Kimberley groped for the chair it would have been wiser to sit in before she had realised the strength of her opponent, who ignored all the rules of civilised combat.

His eyes were on her again, saw she was seated. But he waited no longer to renew his onslaught; his intent, she saw, was to get to the bottom of everything.

'What did you mean last night when you said "The house is mine by right"?' he pursued. 'Is it *this* house you were talking about?'

The fight sustained for so long by the anger he aroused in her had gone, flattened by his brutal reminder that David didn't want her.

'Yes,' she said quietly. And shaking her head, 'I— love this house. My father knew how much I loved Bramcote. And—and yet . . .'

Part of her was no longer with Slade. She was remembering again that deep shock she had felt when Charles Forester had told her the terms of her father's will, the awareness that had been with her of why he had done it.

'And yet?' prompted Slade, making her conscious that he wasn't going anywhere in a hurry, that he had all day to drag everything out of her if need be.

'Under the terms of my father's will,' she said, pulling herself together and eyeing Slade Darville's persistent countenance with intense dislike, 'I could only inherit Bramcote,' her voice faded as she brought out the words Charles Forester had had to repeat to her before they had properly sunk in, 'if my status was that of a married woman on a date six months from the date of my father's death.'

She had gone from Slade, remembering again the shock that had ripped through her that day. Slade brought her sharply back, taking what she had revealed in his stride.

'Fortunate for you I asked you to marry me, wasn't it?' he said sourly.

Kimberley looked at him, seeing no point now in holding anything back. 'I did consider the possibility of doing the proposing myself if you didn't look like doing so,' she told him honestly—and couldn't miss, from the surprise in his face, that this was something he just hadn't been expecting.

'My God!' he breathed. Then, his surprise quickly over, 'May I ask, if you had done the proposing, what you were going to offer as bait? I assume,' his eyes flicked insolently over her, 'the body was not to be part of the bargain.'

She bit her lip. She guessed she had asked for that one. 'I hadn't got round to thinking very deeply about your part in all of it,' she said, that honesty that was bred in her reluctant to leave.

'That much is obvious,' he said shortly—which had her remembering the way he had seemed determined to possess her last night, the way she had fought and struggled with him so that he should not.

But he was waiting to know what she had supposed he was going to get out of it if it had come to it that she had been the one to do the asking. He didn't put the question again of what was she going to offer as bait. But she was learning about him, learning that once he had set his mind on something, he was very determined. And she knew she wasn't leaving this room until he had learned all there was to learn.

'It occurred to me,' she said, that honesty in her preventing her from lying, 'that with you an out-of-work actor, as I thought,' she still hadn't fully accepted that she had married herself to a wealthy man, 'that perhaps it might save your pocket to live here free for a few weeks.' She saw his eyebrows lift at that, but having got started, she went on, stumbling, 'Father didn't—didn't—he only left enough money for me to—well, he didn't leave much in actual cash. But I would have offered you half . . .'

She heard his sharp intake of breath. 'So you weren't after my money!'

'No. I told you I wasn't,' she said, angry that he

could believe that of her.

'No need to get hot and bothered,' said Slade easily. 'Your honesty since this discussion started has me believing you.' He paused, gave time for that to sink in, to cool her rising anger, then asked, 'Why, with your father knowing how you care about . . .' he glanced around him, having the opposite effect of damping down her anger by calling her beloved Bramcote, 'this heap of masonry, did he put the married woman stipulation on your inheriting?'

'Isn't it obvious?' she said snappily.

'So tell me.'

Kimberley glared at him, tempted to walk out right then. But she knew, even as the temptation to do so came, that she might as well get it all over with now. He would only follow her around the house, wherever she went, badgering her with his question. Too late she was beginning to know him. Though it wasn't too late. Didn't she have Bramcote?

Slade returned her glaring look with a steady, unconcerned by her anger look of his own. Damn him, she thought, hating that he was silently waiting. Waiting, knowing she couldn't go anywhere where he couldn't follow.

She sighed, knowing herself helpless. 'My father knew I would never marry. I told him I wouldn't.'

'Because of David Bennet?'

Anguish was with her to hear David's name spoken. Had she mentioned David's surname, or had he heard it from Doreen? Edward? Her meditations were cut short. Slade wasn't waiting for an answer to his question, he had another one ready.

'Why was it so important to your father that you marry?' She didn't like that question any more than she had liked any of his others. But he was pressing on. 'As I understand it, young women these days no longer regard being married as the be-all and end-all.'

He was shrewd, she saw. He had not taken anything

she had told him at face value. He was digging and digging, regardless of any pain he might cause her.

'What's so different about you, Kimberley,' he refused to let up, 'that your father, as devoted to you as you were devoted to him from all I've heard, should think it so imperative that you marry?'

'Damn you!' came firing from her. She'd had enough. Was nothing sacred? 'It's none of your business . . .'

'By marrying me, you've made everything my business,' he fired back ruthlessly.

Electricity charged between them as Kimberley refused to answer and Slade insisted that she should. They weren't going to be married for very much longer, she could see that, so why should she answer? From where she was sitting he looked to be in the same mind as her—that the sooner they were divorced the better.

Yet still he waited for her reply. Her stubbornness wilted. She wanted to be by herself, and there was only one way that was to be achieved.

'If you must know,' she said, the words dragged from her against her will. 'If you must know, my father was over-protective about me.' Now would he be satisfied?

He wasn't. 'What cause had he for being over-protective?' He refused to let up, making her think exasperatedly that a barrister would have been a better calling for him than a stockbroker.

She sighed as the words tugged from her, 'My mother was—highly strung.' Fed up to the back teeth with his questions, despairing of having just her own solitary company ever again, she let him have it all in one go, as she added, 'My father thought I might have inherited some of her highly-strung tendencies.' And going on, kicking all the way, 'When I was ten he insisted, against my mother's wishes, that I was sent away to boarding school. He thought it might toughen me up . . .'

She saw that some of the asperity had gone from Slade, but there was still a question in his eyes. It had her continuing, not waiting for the question to be asked, her voice beginning to falter:

'I—I was back home after a week. During that week I was away m-my mother accidentally drowned.' Silently Slade waited. 'My father blamed himself,' Kimberley added.

A kind of hush fell in the room in the moments it took before Slade's quietly spoken enquiry came.

'He thought that, missing you, she had committed suicide?'

She nodded. 'I'm positive it was accidental,' she said, feeling strangely, much calmer now. 'The area where it happened always had been dangerous. It's fenced off now.'

'So,' he said slowly, 'unsure if your mother's death was suicide, your father kept more than a normal paternal eye on you.'

'Yes,' she admitted, and knew he was waiting for more. 'I can only guess that—that after I showed signs of a nervous breakdown, Dad, knowing his time with us was limited, knowing also how much I love this house—that I would do anything to keep it—thought, he must have done, that a—a husband would take over his role of protecting me after he'd gone.'

Sadness was with her as she came to the end. She had loved her father so much, but oh, how misguided he had been! She might be like her mother in looks, but she had inherited something from her father too. She would have coped without David, as he had learned to cope without his adored Rosemary. She would have managed.

Her sadness was interrupted by Slade. Aggression was back there again, taking no account that he had stripped her bare, as he gritted:

'What a pity for you, dear Kimberley, that my feelings for you come nowhere near to being fatherly.'

'Your feelings for me?' She was rapidly brought out of her melancholy. 'Oh . . .' Memory returned of his hands on her body, her breasts, and she swallowed. Surely he wasn't saying he still fancied her? 'Your feelings are cancelled out now, aren't they?' she asked quickly, then, starting to feel on firmer ground, 'I mean, now you know you've made a mistake. You had no intention of staying married to me for very long anyway, had you . . .' She missed the narrowing of his eyes, and felt things were at last beginning to swing her way as she trotted out, 'Doreen said if you ever married you'd want a divorce as soon as you'd realised what you'd done.' She even managed a smile. 'Don't you think,' she said pleasantly, 'that we might as well divorce now, since we don't have to wait the few weeks it might have taken you to realise you'd made a mistake?'

Slade smiled too—and she just didn't know him well enough not to trust it. 'Did I say,' he asked softly, 'that I considered I'd made a mistake?'

'But you have! Of course you have,' came bolting from her. 'You married me,' she went on hurriedly, 'because you thought you couldn't—er—get into bed with me any other way.' And, not pausing for breath, 'I think we both know now that you—er—are never going to share my bed.' Kimberley felt better for having got that secret knowledge into the open, and tried her smile again. But it was less certain than it had been before when she saw that Slade didn't appear to be too thrilled with what she was saying. But she wasn't ready to stop yet. 'So—so we can divorce,' she said—and, offering him another uncertain smile, 'We can part friends, can't we, Slade? You can divorce me for non-consummation if you wish, and . . .'

'And you'll be quite happy in this dilapidated house,' he said quietly, taking the smile off her face. Then suddenly he was snarling, 'You selfish bitch! You selfish little bitch!' And while she was staring at him open-mouthed he was thundering, 'Wrapped up in your own small cottonwool world—other people's feelings don't matter a damn to you, do they? Nothing matters to you just so long as you get what you want.'

'That's not true!' she protested. Then, aghast, appalled as for one dreadful moment the insane idea came that Slade might—love her—she asked, 'Feelings?' and was dismissing the notion as ridiculous, even as she was adding, 'What do you mean?' and received his confirmation that love for her didn't enter into it.

'It just hasn't occurred to you, has it, that I might have friends, business acquaintances, whom I've told I won't be seeing for a while because I shall be on my honeymoon? You haven't so much as even deigned to consider what I should feel when those same people learn that my marriage is at an end because I couldn't get my wife to consummate the marriage!'

Kimberley hadn't got as far as thinking he would so much as tell anybody else, she had to admit, realising only then that because she wanted it kept such a dark, dark secret, from everyone except Charles Forester, that didn't necessarily mean that Slade was of the same view. And there was no time to dwell on it now, for Slade Darville was in a fine temper when he threw at her:

'Like hell we'll divorce!'

She couldn't believe he was refusing. 'You're saying . . .?' she couldn't go on.

'No female is going to make me look an impotent fool. Just you try it, sweetheart,' he threatened, 'and this marriage will be consummated before you can get another idea!'

Horrified at what he was suggesting, she was out of her chair. 'You'd—*rape* me!' she gasped.

His cynical laugh echoed round the room. 'It wouldn't be rape, wife, I promise you that.'

He thought he could make her—any other way! Far less comfortable with this subject than she had been with any of the others that had come up, Kimberley got off the subject of his expertise in bed as quickly as she could.

'But you've got to divorce me,' she cried, seeing all her plans coming to nothing, and quite forgetful that he had told her he wasn't short of money. 'You can have all the money my father left,' she panicked. 'I'll get a job . . .'

There were granite chips in his eyes as her words reached him. 'I told you I thought you'd married me for *my* money, remember,' was his icy reply.

Temper only he could arouse, unfelt for so long, rioted through her, and was there again, when she told him furiously, 'It's for sure no girl would marry you for your personality!'

Then she had the shock of her life when instead of coming back with the acid she had discovered he was more than capable of, to her astonishment, Slade threw back his head and roared with laughter, controlling his mirth as he found some of her brief pleasantness to murmur:

'Carry on like that, my sweet, and I do believe I'm going to enjoy living here.'

'You mean— you intend to *stay*?' It couldn't be true! Hadn't he understood . . .

'Till death us do part,' he offered silkily, and if he saw the outrage in her face, he took no heed to it as he told her, 'I did have it in mind for us to move into my London home, but, given Bramcote could do with a few major repairs,' his eyes were positively devilish, she thought as he paused, then added, 'it's not such a bad little heap.'

Kimberley threw him a look of loathing as without saying another word she stormed from the study. She had to. Had she stayed she was sure she would have physically attacked him.

She exited through the kitchen door, fuming. Not such a bad little heap! How dared he talk like that about Bramcote! And what major repairs? She remembered a damp patch that had appeared on the landing ceiling that day he had proposed—if you could call it a proposal. The torrential rain must have found its way through a loose slate. She'd get somebody to have a look at it soon. But first she had to get rid of Slade.

Till death us do part! He didn't mean that any more than he had meant his marriage vows. She knew that for a fact. Well, he needn't think she was going to play some game of being the 'little woman'. If he was hungry he could get himself something to eat. She knew the countryside well, she'd be blowed if she'd go home until she was good and ready. Perhaps he'd get tired of waiting, she thought hopefully. Perhaps if she didn't go home until dark she would find him and his swanky car gone.

Had she thought before she had taken off so angrily, then she would have stopped to pick up her purse to buy a bun or something, but she hadn't. And it was at eight o'clock that night and still light, having had nothing in her insides all day, that hunger had a more even-tempered Kimberley on her way back to Bramcote.

But if she had been hoping to find Slade similarly even-tempered, she was doomed to disappointment as she walked up the garden path and into the kitchen. For he was standing there waiting for her, his face grimmer than she had ever seen it, as before she had got the door shut he was demanding:

'And just where in sweet hell do you think you've been?'

To say a sarcastic 'Been pining?' wouldn't go down at all well, she saw, the evenness of temper she had found these last hours beginning to fray at the edges.

'You wouldn't know if I told you,' she answered quietly. 'It would only bore you.'

'Then bore me,' Slade said toughly. 'I've spent the whole of the day searching for you without catching so much as a glimpse of you.'

'You've been looking for me?' Her brow puckered. 'Something has happened?' she asked quickly. 'There's been an accident?' Her mind flew wildly in all directions, her face paling as she wondered if David's father had called from the next village. Had something happened to David?

'Nothing has happened. There hasn't been any accident,' Slade told her bitingly, and was furious with her when, relief flooding in that David was safe, she asked innocently:

'What, then? Why were you looking for me?'

'Selfish bitch was an understatement!' he bellowed, letting go the hold he had on his temper, his hand clenching as he held on to what looked to her to be an urge to knock seven bells out of her. 'When I went through that farcical marriage ceremony yesterday I took over responsibility for you.'

She didn't want him feeling responsible for her, it would foul things up if he thought he could boss her around until such time as she could get rid of him.

'It's not necessary,' she began. 'There was no need at all for you to come looking for me . . .'

'After our discussion this morning I thought there was.'

She frowned again. 'You mean my telling you about my father's . . .'

'I mean about you telling me about your highly strung mother,' he told her flatly, recapturing his short temper as he watched while she got on to the track his mind had gone on.

'You thought . . .' she said, winded, not crediting it. 'You thought with my saying my father had some doubt that she—she hadn't died—accidentally, that I—that I . . .' Slade stood and glowered at her so that she had to finish, 'that I might have committed—suicide?'

She couldn't believe it, but it was the only answer that fitted.

'You were upset when you went out,' he reminded her.

'Yes, but . . .'

'You're just selfish enough to leave me with your suicide on my conscience.'

'Oh, come on,' she retaliated. 'I'll grant even one's worst enemy wouldn't want to live with someone else's death on their conscience for the rest of their lives, but surely you don't think, upset as admittedly I was,' though she had been more boiling over than upset, she recalled, 'that I would go that far just because you're pretending you don't want a divorce?'

Slade didn't answer, which had her wondering if she had given him grounds for thinking she was as highly strung as her mother had been. He knew all about her near-nervous breakdown, the tranquillisers she liked to keep near just in case she couldn't hold out against taking one. But even so . . .

Guilt she didn't want. Compunction came to swamp her that another human being, even not liking her very much as she was sure was the case with Slade— nobody went around calling someone they had any regard for the selfish bitch he had called her a couple of times—should have spent hours worrying that she might have done herself a mischief. It squashed any anger that had been in her, and had her, regardless of his stony expression, wanting him to see she wasn't selfish. Thoughtless maybe, but truly, truly sorry.

'I'm sorry, Slade,' she apologised. 'I never gave it a thought that . . .' she waved a hand in the air helplessly. 'I can see now how it must have looked to you, but . . .' Her need to apologise was wearing thin, because he wasn't prepared to give. 'I'm sorry,' she said, and would have gone from the room, fed up with him and everything else, only he hadn't finished yet.

'In future,' he said, 'whenever you find the need to

wander off on your own, you will remember first to tell me where you're going.'

His high-handed manner offended her. 'Very well,' she said stiffly, and was almost out of the kitchen when he called her back.

'Have you eaten today?'

She was starving, but she wasn't going to admit it if it meant spending more time in his unpleasant company. 'I'm not hungry,' she lied.

'Go and get cleaned up, I'll fix you something.'

'Look here, you,' rocketed from her, 'you may be married to me, but you're not boss in this house!'

'With all my worldly goods,' he quoted, just to aggravate her, she was sure, good humour restored to his face. 'I'll give you fifteen minutes,' he added, good humour disappearing. 'If you're not back by then . . .'

Kimberley didn't wait for any more. She knew that urge to hit out at him might not stay controlled if she was in the same room with him another second. Oh, what had she done?

She washed her face and hands, tidied her hair, and thought of Bramcote. She couldn't regret that she had done what she had, she couldn't. And since she had— at the most, she hoped, a couple of weeks before Slade got fed up with the situation and took himself off— then everything would turn out fine. Just fine.

She even found herself humming cheerfully as she tripped lightly down the stairs. 'Fourteen minutes exactly,' she said brightly as she entered the kitchen and the mouthwatering smell of cooked gammon greeted her nostrils.

'Cut some bread,' she was ordered.

Oh, how she would like to take him down a peg or two! she thought, looking wistfully at the sharp part of the breadknife. She caught him looking at her.

'I don't have murderous intentions too,' she said. And sweetly; 'None that I would have the nerve to carry out,' she qualified, and knew herself confused that she could see the edge of a grin Slade was trying to suppress.

So her sense of humour tickled him, she thought, and had to suppress a smile of her own that, oddly enough, that pleased her.

'That was delicious,' she said, when the gammon and eggs had been demolished with unusual appetite by her. It must be because she had been out in the air all day, she thought. Which was odd again, because there had been days when she had spent hours in tidying up the garden, yet hadn't been able to face food when she had come in.

She thought it was time she did something about taking charge of her kitchen again. 'I'll wash up,' she said when the meal was over. 'No need for you to help.'

Slade took her bossing him about for a change very well, she thought. 'Thank heaven for that,' he said—but couldn't let it go without letting her know who he thought was master. 'You can bring me in a cup of coffee when you've finished. I'll be in the study.'

She wouldn't be angry with him, she wouldn't! Kimberley thought, up to her arms in washing up suds, unwanted thoughts of how fair was she being to him starting to penetrate. Last night she had tried to be fair, tried to give him what he wanted out of this marriage—and look what had happened.

The lack of confidence in her ability to hold a man since David, as Slade had so kindly put it, had jilted her, began to bug her again. But this time she was glad Slade would soon get tired of her. Though since she considered, as in all fairness she had to, that she still owed him something—it wasn't his fault he wasn't the penniless actor she had thought—then the least she could do was to be civil to him. To think a little, and show him she was not the totally selfish person he thought her to be.

Not, of course, that she wanted his good opinion of

her. What a ridiculous idea! She was still scoffing at the notion when, after making the kitchen tidy, she set about making the coffee he wanted.

Telling herself she wasn't going to get uptight when she saw him sitting in her father's chair, Kimberley entered the study with a tray of coffee which held all he had requested.

Slade looked up, his dark eyes staying on her as she cleared a place on the desk to set down the tray.

'You look busy,' she observed pleasantly, seeing the desk that had that morning been clear was liberally strewn with paper work.

'Just keeping my finger on the pulse.' His eyes were still on her. 'I shan't disturb you when I come up to bed,' he told her evenly.

Her heart jumped. At the back of her mind there had been that terrible doubt. Was he saying . . .? 'I'll—I'll have to leave my bedroom lamp on or—or you'll most likely—er—bump into something when you—er—cross to your room,' she managed to get out, her nerves playing up as she waited for his answer. Waited for the confirmation she wanted that it was to that room he would be going—without stopping.

His mouth picked up at one corner, as, deliberately she thought, he kept her on tenterhooks.

'I rather enjoyed the way we used to kiss on parting,' he said, keeping her waiting. 'But—should you be asleep,' he paused, the devil in his eyes, 'then I'll put your lamp out for you, as I pass.'

'I'm a little tired,' she said gravely, not wanting him to see how pleased she was. 'I think I'll go to bed now.'

'Goodnight, Kimberley,' he said, but had her nerves jangling again when a cool hand came out and took hold of her wrist.

For wordless moments she looked at him, not seeing why he should be holding on to her when he had just said goodnight. Then darting in came his comment of not many seconds ago when he had said he liked the way they used to kiss in parting.

He let go her wrist, and fair play tugged at her that he still appeared to be waiting.

'Goodnight,' she said, and warily, not moving, her eyes fixed to his, she stood hesitating. Then quickly, though he could still have made a grab for her and held her had it been in his mind, she bent her head to his and briefly touched her mouth to his.

Quietly she closed the study door after her. Then as if the devil was after her, she raced to her room, for the first time wishing that the house had been planned differently, and that there was another door leading to the dressing room that would have done away with Slade Darville having to cross her room to reach it.

She felt tired, but could not get to sleep. And hours later she was still awake when she heard Slade coming to bed. She closed her eyes, feigning sleep, and cursed the need to leave her bedroom lamp on for him to see his way.

Quietly the door opened, and she heard his firm tread. The door closed. She tried to keep her eyelids from flickering. He moved, she heard him, and then he stopped.

Where was he? Kimberley felt as tense as a coiled spring. Was he near? Was he looking down at her? Perspiration broke out, as her nerves got to her, fear that he was about to touch her. She opened her eyes and saw he was nowhere near.

He was standing by the dressing table, her bottle of tablets in his hand, he had been considering them, but was no longer. He had seen she was awake.

'Thought you were tired,' he remarked.

The lie sprang into her head to tell him she had been asleep and that his coming in had awakened her. But suddenly she found she just couldn't lie to him. Then she didn't have to say anything, for he was looking again at the bottle in his hand.

'How many of these have you taken?' he enquired.

'Tonight,' she answered, 'none. I haven't taken any at all today.'

Slade returned the tablets to the dressing table. But instead of going on to his room, to her consternation he came and sat on her bed.

'That pleases me,' he said. And on seeing how one of her hands was fidgeting with the bed sheet, he took hold of it, feeling her instinctive move to pull it back. 'Now don't get uptight,' he soothed.

'I——' The words to contradict him wouldn't come. What did come were words she hadn't rehearsed, but words which came straight from her need to be free again. 'Divorce me, Slade,' she said urgently—and knew from the way her hand was crushed in his, before she noticed how hard his eyes had gone, that she hadn't chosen a very good moment to remind him he had threatened to consummate the marriage before he would divorce her. 'You can use any grounds you choose,' she added hastily.

He let go her hand, then stood, surveying her pale face from his lofty height. 'If I were you, Kimberley Darville, wanting so desperately to keep all that's yours, I sure as hell wouldn't keep yapping on about divorce.'

Oh God, she thought, swallowing painfully, she had reminded him of his threat. 'You . . .' You wouldn't, she wanted to say, but he would, she knew he would.

'Purify your mind, sweetheart,' he said roughly. 'I wasn't referring to sex.'

Could she believe him? 'W-what then?' she asked shakily.

'It could be that if you go on and on about divorce, I might just take you up on it.'

Well, she'd be putting the bunting up that day, that was for sure! But . . . Suddenly she had an ominous premonition. Confident Slade Darville always was, but from where she was lying, he appeared to be a man who held five aces.

'That should worry me?' she asked slowly.

'It should,' he agreed, going on to say, 'You're an intelligent woman, Kimberley. That being so, you should have realised when I met and married you in three weeks that I don't like to drag my feet when once I've reached a decision.'

If he made a rapid decision about a divorce, so much the better as far as she could see. But she felt something was wrong somewhere, so she did not tell him how enthusiastically she would greet that news.

'So?' she asked, and waited.

'So, my darling,' Slade said sardonically, 'should I decide to change my mind and divorce you, I would move quickly.'

He smiled that smile she had seen once and should never have trusted. It made her even more wary as she waited. And when he revealed what was behind his smile, Kimberley was staggered that the intelligence he had credited her with must have been so dimmed by her need to have Bramcote secured that she had not thought of it herself.

'You could, Kimberley,' he said, savouring every word, 'if you don't shut up about a divorce, find yourself a single woman—*not married*,' he underlined, 'when the six-month anniversary of your father's death arrives.'

CHAPTER FIVE

How could she have overlooked that very vital point? The thoughts that had gone round and around in her brain before sleep had finally claimed her were back with her as soon as Kimberley awakened the next morning.

It turned everything upside down, didn't it? *He* knew that too, the smug devil! She had to put all thoughts of divorcing him out of her head for a while. And what was more, she had to hope with all her heart that her fast-moving husband wouldn't take it into his head to do what less than twelve hours ago she had been ready to beg him to do. One thing she knew, Slade Darville hadn't made himself any more endearing by, without lifting a finger, so successfully turning the tables on her.

Kimberley got out of bed. The dressing room door was closed, which probably meant he was still in the land of dreams. She hoped he stayed there all day.

But on going downstairs, she found him in the kitchen eating the last of the bread in the shape of a piece of toast.

'Sleep well?' he enquired cheerfully.

'Eventually,' she replied, going over and feeling the teapot.

'Proper little ray of sunshine in the morning, aren't you, my sweet?' he commented, munching cheerfully away. 'What time does the paper boy arrive?'

'He doesn't,' she said shortly. Then as he gave her a 'watch it' look, she realised she'd got to make some sort of an effort if she didn't want him divorcing her before February. 'I stopped the papers when my father died.' She had the radio, cutting out newspapers and magazines meant the money could go towards something else.

'Not to worry,' said Slade, getting up from the table. 'I can get one in town.'

'You're going into Thaxly?'

He shook his head. 'London.'

'You're going to see your solicitors?' Her tea slopped over, her nerves shooting at the thought after all this she was going to lose her home.

'Relax, my sweet,' he said, 'You'll be the first to know if I decide to change anything. There are other things in London beside the fastest solicitor on the draw—whom I just happen to have working for me.'

'Oh,' she said, her nerves settling.

He came near. 'Got a kiss for hubby?'

'Do you have to be so cheerful?' she asked, pulling her head out of range.

Slade went without his kiss, but went whistling, disgustingly cheerfully to her mind, out to his car.

Perhaps he wasn't coming back, she thought hopefully as the day wore on. Why she should trust his 'You'll be the first to know if I decide to change things' she didn't know. But peculiar though she found it, she did.

By the time four o'clock came Kimberley started to grow more and more convinced he wouldn't be back. Rain had set in when seven o'clock came and still no sign of him. He wasn't coming back, she was sure of it, she thought, putting the edgy feeling that had been growing in her down to the fact that he could at least have telephoned to say what his plans were.

She wondered if he had put in an appearance at his office that day, although he had intimated he had told one and all he would be on his honeymoon.

He was definitely not coming back, she thought at half past seven. Even if he had been to his office, Amberton was only a little over an hour's run from London. He should have been here by now.

She wasn't hungry, so she went to the living room and stood absently staring out of the window, to see old Sammy, the poacher, go by. She was just about to draw back, not wanting it to look as though she'd got nothing better to do, when she saw Slade's car draw up.

Her first reaction was to come away from the window. But her vision was arrested to see Slade emerge from his car, not in the suit he had left in that morning, but clad in a light sweater and slacks, and he was now stopping to have a few words with old Sammy.

Kimberley was pensive as she left the living room and went to the kitchen. David had never had any time for old Sammy. He had passed him by many a time when she had been with him without so much as giving him the time of day. Not that there was anything wrong in that, she thought, David could do as he liked, though it had momentarily disturbed her that he could pass by one of the few characters the village could boast of, just as though he didn't exist.

Because she was thirsty, and for no other reason, Kimberley put the kettle on. Slade could share her pot of tea if he liked, it was up to him.

She glanced at the door when it was pushed inwards, her eyes staying fixed to it when it was propped open and two mammoth suitcases were pushed inside, their owner following them in.

Good grief! How long did he think he was staying! 'You look as though you intend to stay for the duration,' was out before she could stop it.

'And good evening to you too, dear wife,' replied Slade, a sardonic reminder that she might have greeted him first before she fired her first salvo.

But Kimberley's spirit, that had been fuelled into life these past few days, wasn't yet ready to go into hiding again.

'I was hopeful you weren't coming back at all,' sped from her.

'I can go back again if you would prefer an instant divorce,' was his short answer, deflating her completely.

She turned from him, hating him, glad the kettle was boiling so she was saved a reply. She swallowed down her ire, knowing he had her beaten.

'Do you want a cup of tea?' she offered ungraciously.

'I want more than that,' he said, and she tesed, her hands starting to shake that they were back to *that* subject. Until he tacked on the end, 'I want my dinner. What have you prepared for me?'

'Prepared for you?'

She swung round. She hadn't given a thought that he might want feeding when he came home, yet here he was like some Victorian husband demanding food the moment he set foot inside the door!

'You're saying you have nothing ready?'

'I—wasn't expecting you back,' she said, of necessity quelling the urge in view of his acid comment about an instant divorce to tell him to go to hell.

His reply to that was a grunt as he opened the fridge door. Another grunt was emitted when its contents showed only half a dozen eggs and a pint of milk.

'Where's the rest of your food?'

There was a walk-in larder, but apart from flour and a few other oddments, there was very little in there either.

Kimberley felt herself colour and turned away, embarrassment making her feel too uncomfortable to look him in the eye.

'I—don't need very much,' she mumbled. She felt the cold silence behind her, and didn't like it. It was forcing her to go on when she didn't want to, and she hated him the more for it. 'I—my resources are—limited,' she said, and still wouldn't look at him.

The silence at her back stretched, but still she wouldn't look at him. And then he was asking, 'Just

how much money did your father leave you?' That had
her twisting round in fury at his colossal impudence.
But she saw he was unrepenting that she thought he
had a fine cheek. 'How much?' he repeated, and she
knew he was insisting on knowing.

She could wriggle as much as she liked, but that
dark glimmer in his eyes demanded an answer.
Dragging her feet all the way, quietly, she told him—
saw his eyes widen slightly, and would never forgive
him that his voice was dripping with sarcasm when he
said:

'And you were going to give me *all* of it.'

She came the nearest ever to hitting him then, but
found from somewhere a great strength to resist the
impulse. Then she told him with quiet dignity:

'Money has never been important to me.'

'Not even if the house that *is* important falls about
your ears because you haven't the wherewithal to
maintain it properly?'

'You swine!' she called him, and saw how little her
calling him names affected him, as nonchalantly he put his
hand in his pocket, then tossed her his car keys. Instinc-
tively she caught them.

'Take my car and go and get me some fish and chips,'
he ordered.

Her eyes flew wide. '*Fish . . .?* It's tipping it down
out there!' she protested. Who the hell did he think he
was? 'I'd be soaked before I got to your car!' He stood
there not giving way, making her wish she hadn't
resisted the hot impulse to take a swing at him—
especially when she found herself offering, 'I'll make
you some chips if you like—there are a few potatoes in
the larder.'

'Enough for two?'

So she was going to be made to eat too—and with
him. 'I'll bring it through to the dining room when it's
ready,' she said, intensely irritated—and was even
more irritated to hear his reply, when he was already

putting her to the trouble she wouldn't have bothered with for herself.

'We'll eat in here.'

God, what wouldn't she like to do to him, she thought, when egg and chips had been demolished, her kitchen was looking spruce again, and she went on her way upstairs. But the pleasant picture of seeing him tarred and feathered abruptly disappeared when she reached the landing and saw rain was dripping in through the place that had shown a damp patch the last time they had a downpour.

For an age she stood dithering watching the steady plop, plop of water hitting the carpet. She knew that since all the buckets and bowls, any sort of receptacle to catch the water in, were all in the kitchen, she would have to go down again. Then she did an about-turn hoping Slade had vacated the kitchen where she had left him reading his newspaper.

He was still there. She knew his eyes were on her as wordlessly she found a bowl. She would like to have left him without a word, but had a sudden thought that he might send the bowl emptying its contents all over the carpet if, not expecting an obstruction, he didn't bother putting the landing light on when he came to bed.

'Leak,' she said briefly. 'On the landing.'

Oh, how she wished she hadn't! Not one word did he say. It made her wish she had kept quiet too. It would have been worth a sodden carpet just to hear him measuring his length as he tripped over the bowl, she thought.

In bed, later, she felt less antagonistic towards him. What could he have said? He had already revealed that he thought the whole house was about to collapse. To have added anything to that wouldn't have made her feel any better about the leak.

How long he stayed downstairs, Kimberley had no idea. But having anticipated that she would still be awake when he came to bed, she opened her eyes to find her bedside lamp had been switched off at some time, and that it was now daylight.

Refusing to let her mind dwell on the uncomfortable thought that he had been in her room while she had slept, she was quickly out of bed and donning her dressing gown to go and see how much water the bowl she had placed beneath the leak had collected.

She discovered she wasn't the only one on the same errand. Slade was on another part of the landing, fully dressed, a bucket and cloth at his feet as he mopped up as much excess water as he could from a second leak that had appeared in the night.

'Oh no!' she cried, going over to stand near him.

'Afraid so,' he said, straightening, his eyes going over her figure, slender in her thin wrap. 'It wouldn't surprise me if the roof needs stripping and re-slating.'

'As bad as that?' she said faintly. 'It can't be . . .'

'I observed that it didn't look too sound a couple of weeks back,' Slade remarked. And, quite kindly, 'Men notice these things.'

Kimberley certainly hadn't. Bramcote was just Bramcote, and she loved it. She saw nothing wrong with it, but she had to now, and she just didn't dare think how much a new roof would cost. She pushed shaky fingers through her long tousled hair, and saw that his eyes had followed her movement. She saw admiration there and momentarily, as attacked by alarm, she forgot all about the roof.

'Steady,' Slade advised, a smile showing itself. 'You have a natural beauty, Kim, there's nothing unusual about a man appreciating the fact. It doesn't necessarily mean he's panting to get into bed with you every minute of the day.'

She felt complimented. And as panic died, she realised she must be learning to trust him that he could so easily disperse that panic.

'Why don't you go and get dressed?' he suggested

quietly. 'I'll finish off here while you fix something for breakfast.'

A smile fluttered to her mouth, then faded. 'There are eggs,' she said, 'but—but there isn't any bread.' She expected a frown, but didn't get one.

'Forget breakfast. We'll have coffee, then go and shop in Thaxly.'

Shopping with Slade was an eye-opener. Whereas she had got into the habit, even before her father had died, of buying only what she considered essentials, and then only the smaller size, Slade seemed to think only the giant size of everything would do. Jars of things she thought they would never use were purchased, he even took her with him to the local wine merchants to stock up, not letting her pay a penny towards anything.

The suitcases he had come home with yesterday were a fair indication that he had moved in. The enormous amount of food he purchased told her that not only had he come to stay, but that she had better shake the dust off her cookery books.

But it was when he took her to an electrical wholesalers and ordered a deep-freeze to be delivered, then went to another wholesalers and arranged dates for pre-packed, pre-frozen meat to be delivered, telling her in front of the assistant, 'It will save you going out, darling, if we have supplies in before the bad weather sets in,' that Kimberley realised he was set to stay with her during the winter.

Had he remarked on the weather when passing the time of day with old Sammy yesterday? she wondered. Had Sammy told him they sometimes got cut off when there was snow about?

Kimberley didn't know just how she felt that on the one hand it didn't look as though Slade was going to take any immediate steps to get a quick divorce, yet on the other, he didn't seem likely to go before spring came.

She was quiet in the car going home, realising she couldn't have it both ways. If she wanted to keep Bramcote, and that was still her dearest wish, then she had a situation on her hands that she had to put up with. Yet was it fair, when that date in February arrived, the house safely hers, that she should then tell Slade she had put up with him for long enough? That she should then tell him if he didn't divorce her, then she would divorce him? He would have every justification then for calling her a selfish bitch, wouldn't he?

There was relief from the nagging conscience that plagued her when they arrived back at the house, and Kimberley saw Dr Ellis's car parked outside. They were half way up the garden path, Slade having seen the car too and telling her they would unload later, when she saw Dr Ellis must have decided to try the back door on getting no reply from the front, and had just turned from the kitchen door and was watching her and Slade approaching.

'Hello, Kimberley.'

He was the first to speak, Kimberley having lost her tongue as it came to her that somehow she was going to have to introduce Slade, who, having been the one to lock up when they left, still had the key and was inserting it in the lock while at the same time eyeing the doctor with some speculation.

'G-good morning, Dr Ellis,' she said, feeling decidedly ill at ease—and unnecessarily, since there was nothing wrong with Slade's hearing, 'Slade, this is Dr Ellis.' She saw an eyebrow lift as without introducing him as her husband, she completed, 'Dr Ellis, Slade Darville.'

'Come in, won't you?' It was Slade who did the inviting. Kimberley avoided the doctor's quick surprised look and led the way inside.

Nervous, wanting Dr Ellis out and quickly, uncertain of Slade, she didn't offer the doctor the coffee she normally might have done.

'The—er—'flu epidemic in the village is over, is it?' she asked into what she felt to be a tense silence. Dr Ellis was looking as though he was wondering what was going on.

'It was a stomach ailment,' he corrected her.

'Oh yes,' she said, not surprised she had got mixed up. 'You won't be so rushed now.' She smiled, infected Dr Ellis with her smile so that he forgot Slade and smiled back. Kimberley thought if she made coffee it would give her something to do, but that would mean having to prolong his stay, if he accepted, of course.

'No,' said the doctor, 'I'm still busy, naturally, but I do now have a few minutes I can call my . . .'

'You practise locally?' Slade interrupted.

'In the village,' Colin Ellis replied, and his eyes back on Kimberley, he smiled again. 'How are you, Kimberley?' he asked.

Slade made a small movement, which drew her eyes to his. The look in those dark blue ones that looked not at her, but squarely at the doctor, had her forgetting what the doctor's question to her had been. Slade was about to say something she didn't want him to say. She knew it, just as she knew she was totally powerless to stop him from saying or doing anything he had decided upon.

'I . . .' she began quickly, and found as her voice dried, that Slade was having no such difficulty.

'Tell me, Dr Ellis,' he asked pleasantly, 'was that question about Kimberley's health merely a courtesy, or,' he glanced her way, saw from the look she threw him that she wanted him to shut up, 'was it a professional one?' He smiled at the doctor, that smile that made her wary since it didn't reach his eyes. 'Are you,' he said charmingly, 'by way of being my wife's physician?'

'*Wife?*' Dr Ellis was astounded, she could see that as his eyes rapidly went from Slade to her. 'You're— Kimberley, you're not married to this man, are you?'

LOVE BEYOND REASON
There was a surprise in store for Amy!

Amy had thought nothing could be as perfect as the days she had shared with Vic Hoyt in New York City—before he took off for his Peace Corps assignment in Kenya.

Impulsively, Amy decided to follow. She was shocked to find Vic established in his new life. . .and interested in a new girl friend.

Amy faced a choice: be smart and go home. . .or stay and fight for the only man she would ever love.

MAN OF POWER
Sara took her role seriously

Although Sara had already planned her escape from the subservient position in which her father's death had placed her, Morgan Haldane's timely appearance had definitely made it easier.

All Morgan had asked in return was that she pose as his fiancée. He'd confessed to needing protection from his partner's wife, Louise, and that part of Sara's job proved easy.

But unfortunately for Sara's heart, Morgan hadn't told her about Monique. . .

Your Romantic Adventure Starts Here.

THE LEO MAN
"He's every bit as sexy as his father!"

Her grandmother thought that description would appeal to Rowan, but Rowan was determined to avoid any friendship with the arrogant James Fraser.

Aboard his luxury yacht, that wasn't easy. When they were all shipwrecked on a tropical island, it proved impossible.

And besides, if it weren't for James, none of them would be alive. Rowan was confused. Was it merely gratitude that she now felt for this strong and rugged man?

THE WINDS OF WINTER
She'd had so much— now she had nothing

Anne didn't dwell on it, but the pain was still with her—the double-edged pain of grief and rejection.

It had greatly altered her; Anne barely resembled the girl who four years earlier had left her husband, David. He probably wouldn't even recognize her—especially with another name.

Anne made up her mind. She just had to go to his house to discover if what she suspected was true. . .

These FOUR free Harlequin Romance novels allow you to enter the world of romance, love and desire. As a member of the Harlequin Home Subscription Plan, you can continue to experience all the moods of love. You'll be inspired by moments so real...so moving...you won't want them to end. So start your own Harlequin Romance adventure by returning the reply card below. <u>DO IT TODAY!</u>

EXTRA BONUS
MAIL YOUR ORDER
TODAY AND GET A
FREE TOTE BAG
FROM HARLEQUIN.

BUSINESS REPLY CARD

First Class   Permit No. 70   Tempe, AZ

Before she could answer, Slade had moved to come to stand by her. 'It is a surprise, isn't it?' he remarked blithely. 'It was a surprise to us too, wasn't it, my darling?'

And there still wasn't time for her to get a word in, even if she could have thought of anything suitable. For the staggered look was leaving the doctor, his colour that had blanched at Slade calling her 'my darling' turned to red, as he, most unprofessionally, she thought, exclaimed heatedly:

'You idiot, Kimberley! You stupid idiot!' And, his face working, 'There was no need to marry the first man who asked you in order to comply with the terms of your father's will.'

It was her turn to look astounded. 'You know—about my father's will?' she exclaimed. And while it was still sinking in that he must do since he had been the first to mention it, she felt Slade's arm come around her shoulders, and was too stupefied to think of trying to shake it off.

'The will my wife's father left has nothing at all to do with Kimberley and me being married,' he told him curtly. 'Kimberley married me because she fell in love with me, and for no other reason,' and, his voice changing, 'isn't that right, sweetheart?'

The pressure about her shoulders increased. 'Yes,' she said, not sure if it was pride that said no one was to know the true state of affairs, or if it was because since she had married him he commanded her loyalty in public.

'So you see, Dr Ellis, you have no call to call my wife an idiot. And stupid though she may appear in your eyes for having married me I'm afraid I can't agree with your diagnosis.'

And while Kimberley's mind was boggling that Slade appeared to be taking Dr Ellis severely to task, dropping traces of all but the barest civility, he then sent her anger soaring—anger she was powerless to

release, having let the doctor believe she loved her
husband, as he went on to tell him:

'From now on I will accept full responsibility for
my wife's health. You will kindly oblige me by remov-
ing her name from your list of patients.'

For several blank seconds Colin Ellis looked at him
as if he suspected his hearing was faulty. Then, re-
covering, he turned from Slade, and manfully standing
his ground asked:

'Is this what you want, Kimberley?'

That hard pressure about her shoulders came again.
'I . . .' she began. The pressure on her shoulders didn't
let up. 'Yes,' she said, and felt dreadful at the hurt
look on the doctor's face. She wanted to say such a lot
more. Dr Ellis had been marvellous with her father.
'I'm . . .' she had been going to say 'sorry', but that
bruising weight across her shoulders increased again.

But she didn't have to endure it for very long. Slade
waited only to see the doctor marching off down the
garden path, then he took his arm away.

Which was just as well, because Kimberley had
never been so angry in her life, and felt she would
have severely injured him somewhere had he insisted
on keeping hold of her. As it was, free to move about
as she was, she didn't let a moment pass before she
was rounding on him.

'Who the *hell* do you think you are?' she yelled.

'Don't you know, darling?' he replied, not a scrap
put out, seeming if anything to enjoy seeing the sparks
that were flashing from her in her fury. 'I'm your husband.' And she had been thinking it would be unfair
to ditch him if he was still around in February!

'And you think that gives you the right to . . .' she
started to blaze.

'It gives me *every* right,' he interrupted her sharply,
which she didn't care for any more than she cared for
the implication behind his words. But he hadn't
finished yet, and her anger gave way to utter astonish-

ment when he added, 'And if your doctor friend ever dares to come sniffing around here again, I shall immediately take steps to have him struck off.'

'Struck off?' She was gaping, trying to keep up with him, growing offended at his choice of words. 'What do you mean "sniffing around"?' she challenged disagreeably. 'You know Dr Ellis is ...'

'For an intelligent woman, Kimberley,' said Slade, cutting her off again, 'there are times when you show a distinct lack of brain power.'

'Thanks very much,' she said tartly, that being all she had time for.

'It was clear to me from the moment I saw the way he looked at you,' Slade carried on, stepping over her sharp 'thank you'.

'What was?' She wouldn't stay down. 'What are you talking about?'

He eyed her levelly, causing her to wonder what it was he knew that she didn't. Then suddenly, her bewilderment there in her face to be seen, Slade's aggression left him.

'You had no idea, had you,' he said, 'that he's in love with you?'

Her eyes widened, then scornfully she laughed. 'Don't be ridiculous! I've known him over a year and ... He was marvellous with my father, called every day and never ...'

'Which all adds up,' Slade chopped her off again. Then, leaning indolently against the kitchen sink, 'Didn't it ever occur to you, sweet Kimberley, that it was more than a trifle odd for your father to make the will he did?'

'Odd?' she frowned. She knew full well why her father had left the will he had. She had explained to Slade all about it. 'Odd in what way?' she asked, puzzled.

'You loved your father,' Slade stated gently, 'which is probably why you never thought to question any-

thing about his last bequest. But I never had the
pleasure of knowing the man who reared you.' He was
talking to her kindly, cooling any anger she had felt
with him. 'It hit me straight away as peculiar to say
the least that a man who loved his daughter the way I
believe he loved you should make that stipulation
about you being married before you could inherit the
home you care so deeply for. Particularly,' he added,
his tone not changing when she looked ready to have a
go at him if he was daring to criticise her father, 'when
neither during his illness nor at the time of his death
were you so much as dating anyone, let alone being
near to becoming engaged.'

Her brow puckered as his last words sank in. What
was he implying? She coupled what he had just said
with his remarks about Dr Ellis being in love with
her—and just couldn't believe it.

'You mean he thought . . .' she began incredulously,
'the doctor . . .?'

'Precisely. Your father knew he was going to die. And
I'm confident he must have revealed his worries about
your future to the man who came to the house every day.
Whereupon the doctor told him he had no need to worry,
that he would marry you and take care of you.'

'No,' said Kimberley, shaking her head, not crediting a word of it. That was until Slade said:

'Your father believed you when you said you would
never marry, and knew there was one way to force your
hand.'

All but collapsing at his summing up of the few facts
she had given him, Kimberley reached to the nearest
kitchen chair. She was aware that Slade had taken a
seat near her, but was groping to find a flaw in what
looked like a watertight case.

'But——' she raised her head to see him carefully
watching her every action. 'But,' came slowly from her,
'I would never have married the doctor—I like him
too much.'

'Thanks for nothing,' said Slade with sarcastic charm.

'Oh, you know what I mean!'

'Tell me.'

She knew Slade didn't have any feelings for her but that sexual need to possess her, but suddenly that sensitivity in her knew hesitation in case she touched a nerve. Though why that should bother her, particularly when he had been such a bossy brute, was beyond her.

'Well—with you,' she began, and hesitated, 'er—I don't mean to be unkind,' she said quickly, 'but I don't know you—haven't known you all that long. A divorce wouldn't affect either of us emotionally, would it? Whereas, having known the doctor longer, and . . . and if as you say he is—in love with me, though I'm sure you're mistaken there,' she looked away as she added, 'well, I just couldn't divorce him, could I? I'd—I'd be . . .'

'Stuck with him?' Slade finished for her.

She nodded, unable to look at him again. She knew she hadn't offended him, he knew the score as well as she did. But she had rather revealed too much of her hand. She wouldn't have been surprised to hear some stinging comment on her selfishness— he wouldn't have missed the intimation of what was in her mind come February. But it wasn't he who got mad, but she, when eventually his reply came.

'And what makes you think, dear Kimberley, that you aren't stuck with me?' he enquired blandly.

'You know the answer to that as well as I do!' she snapped as her sparking hazel eyes flew to his cool dark blue ones.

She didn't like it that he was making her feel selfish, when with his track record he would soon get tired of waiting around anyway. Determinedly she turned her mind away from herself and Slade and any guesswork as to how long the marriage might last.

'Anyway,' she challenged, 'what did you mean about having Dr Ellis struck off—you can't dictate like that, as bossy as you are!'

He ignored her opinion on his bossy nature and sent her an insincere smile instead. 'Couldn't I?' he queried softly. 'Not even if the medical bodies got to hear he had amorous intentions towards one of his patients?'

'But he's never laid a finger on me that way!' she protested, gasping anew. Then her eyes gave her away as she remembered that day of her father's funeral, the day Dr Ellis had put an arm round her and touched her cheek with his mouth.

'Are you sure about that?' Slade asked, his voice hardening.

'He kissed my cheek on the day of my father's funeral,' she muttered, too dazed at the thought that Slade could be right in his summing up to think of lying.

Dr Ellis had asked her to call him by his first name too, she recalled. He had made a point of asking her if she was going to Doreen Gilbert's party, said he would look forward to seeing her. Would he, if that stomach bug hadn't kept him busy night and day, have followed it up from there? Had he given her a couple of weeks to get over the initial sorrow of her father's death before . . .

Wide-eyed, she looked at Slade. 'It wasn't a kiss really,' she said, trying to deny that he was right, 'more a . . .'

'Get the picture?' he asked, his voice mocking. 'The warm-up procedure.' And, his voice taking on a sarcastic edge, 'Beginning to regret you made a grab for the first likely-looking candidate you saw?'

His sarcasm brought her out of her stupor. 'Don't tempt me,' she said. Then, truthfully, 'Anyway, I've already told you I wouldn't have married him—even if what you've said is true.'

'Because you think he would have proved more

difficult to get rid of than me?' She didn't answer. 'Lady,' said Slade, 'as you remarked a few minutes ago—you just don't know me.' And on the same breath, 'What are you going to get me for my lunch?'

'How does an arsenic sandwich appeal?' she asked sweetly.

His roar of laughter followed her as she exited from the kitchen, his, 'I'm afraid, my darling, you're going to have to keep me alive. That will stipulated you should be married, not widowed,' ringing in her ears.

The short burst of temper that had had her storming away from his baiting tongue fled, as up the stairs and on the landing, she saw another leak had appeared.

She went downstairs for another bowl, glad to see Slade was out at the car bringing the groceries in, sparing her the need of another of his not so pleasant remarks about the house falling down. The bowl securely in place, she went disconsolately to her bedroom, found pencil and paper, and scratched her head to try to come up with some agreeable figures.

She was still there three-quarters of an hour later, a despondent look in her eyes, when Slade came into the room. If he had come up demanding his lunch then he could take a run, she thought, more pressing matters on her mind.

He observed the pencil and paper still in her hand as he came over to where she was sitting, casually enquiring:

'What are you doing?'

'Your stomach will have to wait,' she said shortly. Then thinking he might know as he looked over her shoulder at her jottings, 'How much do you think a roof repair would cost?'

'More than you've got there, by the look of it,' he said, his cheerful tones grating in her ears. Then, bossing her about again, 'Come and have your lunch. I don't see why mine should go cold as well as yours.'

CHAPTER SIX

HAD she not had the worry of the leaking roof on her mind, Kimberley might well have enjoyed the meal Slade had prepared. Although the mashed potatoes were a touch on the lumpy side, the peas and chops were cooked just right. And he needn't have bothered at all, she thought, her coldness with him vanishing as he ignored her protest that she could do the washing up, and came to give her a hand.

'That the lot?' he asked, looking ready to dump the tea towel.

Kimberley nodded, looking out of the window at the rain that had now fined down to a drizzle so he should not see the smile that wanted to show itself that he found drying up a chore he could do without. But her head swung round in surprise when she heard him suggest:

'Let's take a walk.'

'It's raining!' she protested, not sure he was serious.

His smile was full of charm. 'So wear your wellies,' he said.

Mad—he was quite mad, she thought some ten minutes later when up to her ankles in mud, glad of her wellington boots, Slade in gumboots, they squelched over the rain-sodden paths.

And she must be mad too, she thought, for, suddenly she was enjoying it. Though what she looked like in her stout raincoat and headscarf, she didn't like to think. Slade was bareheaded, seeming not to mind at all that his head was getting soaked, his sturdy trench coat protecting his broad shoulders from the unrelenting drizzle.

And it was outside, Bramcote getting farther and

farther away, that Kimberley found she was talking to
Slade more naturally then she had at any other time.
There was no need to pretend with him any more, she
realised as they squelched on and he helped her over a
stile. Slade knew why she had married him, knew
everything there was to know about her. What was
there to pretend about?

She pointed out places where she used to play as a
child, laughing as she recalled and showed him just
where in the shallow stream she had fallen one day,
and recounted how she had run home waterlogged.

'My friends from those days are scattered all over
the world now,' she told him, 'but we still keep in
touch by mail.'

'Was Bennet a local lad?' he enquired easily.

'He—came from the next village,' she said stiffly,
her pleasure in the afternoon gone. She wished he
hadn't reminded her of David. She hadn't thought
about him at all that day.

Slade stopped, and so did she. He put a damp hand
under her chin, forcing her to look at him. 'Keep your
memories if they're precious,' he said quietly, with
understanding she hadn't expected of him, 'but don't
let them live with you so that the rest of your life
becomes spoilt.'

Solemnly she stared at him. Then suddenly his
mouth was curving upwards, and he was telling her,
'Your husband wants a cup of tea, woman.'

They were both quiet on the way back, and by the
time they reached Bramcote, Kimberley was on the
way to forgiving him for bringing up David's name.
Slade had given her food for thought too. She would
never forget David and those memories that were hers,
but had the time come when she should get down to
thinking what she should do with the rest of her life? It
had seemed too much of an effort at one time to do
more than cope with getting through one day at a time,
but...

Slade opening the garden gate had her aware they had reached home without her knowing it. She remembered he had mooted a cup of tea, and went to put the kettle to boil while she got out of her wet things.

'I'll see to that. You go and get into a hot bath,' Slade said behind her. 'And don't forget to dry yourself well.'

His ordering her about on top of his directing her thoughts away from David, got through to her. And Slade Darville was just too much.

'*You* go and get into a hot bath—and stop bossing me around!' she snapped, her eyes sending daggers at him as she thumped the kettle down and turned to face him.

'What have I done?' he breathed.

And the next moment he was right up to her, had taken her into his arms, looked down at her damp and glowing face for endless moments. Then very gently he removed her sodden headscarf, that hand still gentle as he brushed strands of hair back from her face. Then the next she knew he had pulled her until she was up against him, making no attempt to kiss her as he held her, her head to his chest, his hand keeping it there.

'Take it easy,' she heard him say softly.

Why she should relax against him Kimberley hadn't a clue. But a sigh escaped her as she realised she flew off the deep end so much just lately, it was as if she was trying to make up for all those months when nothing had touched her, moved her.

Slade's hand came to the small of her back, but, afterwards not quite believing it, Kimberley didn't panic. He moved his hand away, not commenting that she hadn't pushed at him, but drew back to show her his hand was wet from contact with her wet raincoat.

Dark eyes looked deeply into her submissive hazel ones. 'You wouldn't like me to have your pneumonia on my conscience, would you?' he asked softly. Like a lamb Kimberley went up to run a hot bath.

What had happened to her down there? she wondered, having come to life in her tub. She shook her head as though to clear it. Slade could be nice sometimes. But that didn't mean she didn't have to be wary of him.

She opened the small drawer in her dressing table, to find a fresh hanky. The bottle of tablets she had returned there when tidying up looked back at her, and she picked it up. Dared she get rid of them? Was she so dependent on a bottle of tablets that she needed them there for insurance?

The bedroom door opening had her head jerking to it before she had come to any conclusion. Slade came in, like herself changed into dry clothes; he had most likely been in and out of the dressing room while she had been in the bath, she thought. Only the dampness of his hair, a shade darker than fair, reminded her of that walk in the rain.

She saw his glance go to the bottle in her hand, saw his mouth tighten as unspeaking he came within a few feet of her, and she knew then from the harsh look in his face what he was thinking. He was thinking, she was sure of it, that the moment downstairs when he had pulled her to rest in his arms had had her needing something to quieten her nerves. And the trouble was, if she didn't want to invite more of the same, only with a more lover-like tendency, then she couldn't tell him he was wrong.

Without saying a word, he gave her one more look, then disappeared into the bathroom to return carrying a glass of water which, still unspeaking, he handed to her.

Kimberley put the glass down on the dressing table and found her voice. 'I wasn't going to take one,' she said, and, niggled that from his sceptical look she could see he didn't believe her, 'I was going to throw them away,' she said, not sure herself if it was the truth or

not. That sceptical look was still there. She went farther. 'I haven't taken any since . . .' she began, and
stopped.

'Since that night I upset your—equilibrium?' he
queried, and made her wish she had dropped them
back in the drawer and slammed it shut when he had
come in, when he drawled, 'You don't think you might
be taking a risk by throwing all of them away?'

For a moment she wasn't with him. And then it hit
her that he was hinting she might need to keep one by
her in case the same thing, his endeavour to consummate their marriage, happened again. She tensed,
choking rather than swallow and let him see how easily
he could flatten her.

'No risk whatsoever,' she said, her words spirited,
only her choky voice betraying her. To prove her
words she took the tablets into the bathroom, un-
screwing the cap as she went, then flushed every last
one of them away.

She knew Slade had followed her in, had watched
her action, when even before she turned to see him
idly resting against the doorpost, she heard his sardonic
drawl:

'And her without a doctor too!'

She brushed past him, went to slam the empty bottle
down on her dressing table as she fought for control.
'You're asking for a punch in the eye!' she said hotly.

And then she had to wonder what was happening to
her, when witnessing Slade's broad grin at her comment, she could do no other than grin in reply.

Then there was nothing of a grin about either of
them. The air was charged as his mouth straightened,
his eyes on her mouth, on her face—it was the first
time he had seen her grin impishly. She saw his jaw
move, saw his hands clench. Then, if he had been
searching for control, control was his.

'You do choose your moments, wife,' he said, then
growled, 'Let's get out of here.'

Because lunch-cum-breakfast had been early, Kimberley decided dinner would have to be early too. For herself she wouldn't have bothered, a meal like the one she had eaten at lunchtime was more than enough to last her a full day. But Slade wouldn't hesitate to demand food when he became hungry. And anyway, since he had cooked lunch, it seemed only fair she should attend to dinner.

He came into the kitchen just as she was putting potatoes to boil. 'How long before dinner?' he enquired, making her glad she had started on the meal without waiting for a nudge from him, since from his remark she guessed he was starving.

'About half an hour.'

'Good. That gives me time to go into the village for a paper. Anything you'd like?'

'No, thanks,' she threw over her shoulder, but watched from the kitchen window his confident stride as he went up the path to the gate.

He was soon back, a paper in one hand, a box of chocolates which he gave to her in the other.

She took them, thanking him, not sure she wanted him buying her presents. The food he had purchased that day she had found excuses for accepting in that it was mainly for him, likewise the freezer he had ordered, though she would make sure he arranged for that to go when he went.

'You shouldn't have,' she said, her face showing she wasn't too happy at his gift.

'Don't make a production of it,' he told her easily, 'or you'll make me regret the impulse. Mind if I sit in here and read until dinner is ready?'

He was actually asking *permission* about something! Mischief flickered into life. 'You'd be more useful if you laid the dining room table,' she said, not looking at him.

There was silence, and she knew he was looking at her, though she hoped he wasn't aware she was about to laugh. 'I married a shrew,' he said, and Kimberley came very near to collapsing in giggles when he dropped his paper on to the kitchen chair and headed for the dining room.

'Okay, so you're right-handed,' Slade said, when as they sat down to their meal he observed the way she changed over the place setting he had laid.

A smile tugged. She was sure he knew that. 'You can't be perfect at everything,' she said—and had to let the smile out when he said on an exaggerated sigh: 'I know, but I *do* try.'

The meal progressed fairly amicably, though Kimberley had long moments of being silent. She found herself wondering why, when up until recently she had seemed to spend so much time in crying, her smile should suddenly be so much freer. Perhaps that initial pain of losing her father was easing, she thought.

But her smile was nowhere to be seen when on leaving the dining room, without waiting for Slade to offer with the washing up she told him she would see to it.

'I know you're dying to get to your paper,' she said.

'I can wait,' he said, following her into the kitchen. 'I've ordered newspapers to be delivered morning and evening, by the way,' he told her.

Abruptly Kimberley halted so that he very nearly walked into her. 'What name did you give at that paper shop?' she asked, moving away, hopeful that he had given her maiden name.

'My own, naturally,' he replied, holding the glance she flicked at him. That grin she had seen in the bed-room was there again as he told her, knowing full well, she thought, that she didn't want anyone to know she had married him, 'No need to worry about your re-putation. I told them Miss Kimberley Adams was now my wife.'

His grin didn't have the same effect of flushing out hers as it had previously. 'You're too good for me,' she retorted sourly.

'True,' he replied unabashed. 'But you're improving.'

Once the washing up was done they went into the living room, Slade taking with him the paper he had bought. Kimberley picked up a book, but couldn't settle. Without a word or excuse, she left the room. It had stopped raining now, and she had her fingers crossed as she went upstairs that the leaks had stopped dripping.

She emptied bowls, but placed them back in position again just in case it came on to rain during the night. Then stood looking up at the ceiling, a despairing feeling coming over her that it might cost a thousand or more to put the roof in any sort of order.

A thousand pounds, she thought dejectedly. She hadn't got that sort of money. They were heading in for winter too. There had been times last year when they had had over a foot of snow. Would the roof take that sort of weight?

If she thought her figures would have come out differently she would have gone in search of paper and pencil and done her sums again. But they wouldn't. And what she could scrape together wouldn't be enough. Slade had known that just by looking over her shoulder.

It was all right for him, she thought, aggrieved all at once that he had money and she didn't. A thousand pounds was neither here nor there to him. She looked at the ceiling again, wondering how long it would take to dry out. Never, if the sun didn't soon show itself, she thought, fed up.

Kimberley took her eyes from the ceiling, thinking she had better go back downstairs. She just wasn't in the mood for any of Slade Darville's sarcasm if he came looking for her. She knew she was in just the right frame of mind for all-out warfare if he said just one word that caught her on the raw.

He looked up from his paper as she went back into the room, but she didn't feel like looking at him. She picked up the book she hadn't found any interest in earlier, and sat down holding it in front of her, but making no attempt to read, her mind still on the impossibility of having that roof repaired before winter set in.

'Something troubling you?'

The quietly voiced question made her jump, made her snappy. 'You could say that,' she replied shortly, dropping her book and all pretence of reading as she stared hostilely at him.

'Tell me about it,' Slade invited evenly. And when she just stared mulishly at him, 'I'll help if I can.'

'You don't mean that,' she said, knowing she was being disagreeable just for the sake of it, but her worries were gigantic, and she was unable to force herself to something she wasn't feeling.

'Try me,' he suggested, unruffled.

Stubbornly Kimberley looked at him, no intention in her of telling him anything. She thought he would get fed up waiting for her answer, and go back to his paper. Then she recalled, when he didn't, that interview with him in her father's study that first morning after their marriage. He had looked then ready to wait for ever to get the answer he wanted. He had that same look to him now.

'The roof leaks,' was dragged out of her.

'I had noticed,' he remarked mildly.

She glared at him, but saw it had not the slightest effect. He was waiting again—waiting for her to say more.

'It's . . .' Damn him! 'I think it will cost about a thousand pounds to have it seen to,' came spilling out. 'I can't afford to have it mended, let alone re-roofed as I suspect wants doing.'

Slade's reply was prompt. 'So how can I help?'

He could have suggested a loan, for one thing,

Kimberley thought mutinously. And on that thought, before she could stop them, the words were falling, no chance of bringing them back:

'It wouldn't hurt you to lend me the money,' she snapped. Then, aghast at what she had just said, 'Forget it,' she said quickly, hot colour of embarrassment colouring her skin.

'We won't forget it,' he said tersely, his eyes watching her fluctuating colour. 'You do too much of bottling everything inside you—that's probably half the cause that led you to the valium belt.'

'Thank you, doctor!' she flashed.

But Slade didn't rise again, except to say, 'Let your worries out, Kimberley,' he said nothing. But sat there favouring her with that steady waiting look that had her dropping her eyes. Had her wanting to scream at him to leave her alone. To leave her alone to work things out for herself.

But she had already tried that and come up without an answer—where else was there to turn? She flicked a glance at him again, saw he was still waiting, and had to admit he defeated her.

She sighed, though whether from exasperation with him she knew not. 'All right,' she said tiredly, 'I'll try it your way.' But she didn't, for a moment, know where to begin. Then she caught his encouraging look. 'I don't think the roof is going to last through the winter, and that troubles me. If the roof goes, the ceilings will come down, and that worries me. But, at the rate I can save, it will take me a couple of years to pay to have it fixed, and that worries me dreadfully, b-because the roof,' her voice tailed off, 'won't last that long.'

'So the answer you think is for me to pay to have it fixed?'

His voice had sounded thoughtful, as though he wasn't dismissing the idea out of hand, and from the depths of despair Kimberley knew sudden hope. She hadn't meant it when she had first blurted out that it wouldn't hurt him to lend her the money, but if he was going to take her up on it, for the sake of dear, dear Bramcote, she knew she just wasn't going to refuse.

'It would only be a loan,' she said, eagerness replacing the flat feeling that had been in her. 'I'd pay you back, every penny.'

'I'm sure you would,' he said, his look sincere, just as though he had learned something about the honesty in her despite that initial deception she had practised, then had her fighting not to go down when he added, 'But you would beggar yourself to do that, and that just isn't on.'

'Why?' she objected; having felt the money for the roof within her grasp she was not ready to let go. 'Why isn't it . . .'

'Because apart from anything else,' Slade told her, a tough look coming to him as he denied her request, 'while you were scratching around to repay me, you would have nothing in hand to cover the next lot of repairs.'

'What repairs?' It had been brought home to her that the roof was bad, but there was nothing wrong with the rest of the house, she thought, bridling that just because he didn't see Bramcote the way she did, he was sitting there unconcernedly finding fault with it.

His voice was kind, although he couldn't have missed the way she was ready to fly at him. 'You love your home,' he said. 'I have good reason to fully appreciate just how much it means to you.' Some of her anger died at his referring to the sole reason she had married him. 'But loving the old place as you do,' fire lit her eyes again at the way he referred to Bramcote as 'the old place', but Slade ignored it as he went on, 'you just haven't seen it as I, a newcomer, have seen it.'

Kimberley swallowed down her anger. Slade had

only ever played fair with her. He wouldn't lie to her now just for the sake of it. That acknowledgement brought with it the thought how less than fairly she had played.

'What,' she said chokily, knowing as unfair as she realised she was being, she still couldn't give him what he had married her for, 'do you, with your newcomer's eyes, see as wrong with it?'

Oh, how she wished she hadn't asked! 'Aside from several minor repairs the local odd job man could see to, the electric wiring has just about had it. Inside those two years you spoke of the house is going to need to be rewired. And leaving aside the plumbing, which is— tolerable,' he told her, 'the walls of the room I sleep in have perished . . .'

'Perished?'

'It's only the wallpaper that's keeping the plaster up,' he said. 'The...'

'Don't go on!' She was appalled. It was true nothing had been done to the house for years, but . . . She left off thinking about Bramcote, colour flushing her cheeks again as she visualised the excellent plumbing, plastering and leak-free roof in the home he had in London. And she couldn't look at him; her pride in the dust as she said huskily, 'You think the house I love is a slum, don't you?'

'No, I don't,' he told her firmly, lifting her pride up off the floor. 'I think Bramcote is a house with great potential, great charm.'

Her pride was back, and it stiffened her. 'But not charming enough for you to dip your hand into your millions to lend me a measly thousand?' she queried, hostile again.

Slade's mouth quirked, not making her feel any better disposed to him. She might just as well have kept her worries to herself. She certainly wasn't feeling any better for having aired them. By telling her what was wrong with Bramcote, he had only added to them.

'Hardly millions,' he said casually, admitting, 'Though I wouldn't miss a *measly* thousand, just the same. But even so, Kim,' his shortening of her name didn't soften the, 'I will not lend you the money,' that followed.

Pride like a banner before her, Kimberley stood up. 'Thank you, Slade,' she said bitterly, 'for giving the matter your full consideration. I assure you I feel on top of the world since I offloaded my worries and consequently discovered what a ruin I'm living in!'

She would have sailed past him then with her nose in the air—had she had the chance. But she didn't. Slade was on his feet too, commanding her to sit down. She ignored him, managed perhaps two steps to the door, then had her eardrums shattered as temper came to him at her airy disdain.

'*Sit down!*' he barked. And, some control returning, 'My God, don't you ever stay to finish a discussion?'

Kimberley didn't like at all that at his roar she had obeyed his order. She was thoroughly disgruntled to find she had collapsed at his bellowing at her into the nearest seat at hand.

'What else is there to discuss?' she asked, loathing him for mastering her.

His voice had quietened, though it was some moments before he spoke, his eyes still glinting with the remains of his wrath, the dark blue now navy.

'I've told you I will not lend you the money to have the roof fixed,' he said levelly, 'and I stand by that.' He broke off, looking at her as if weighing his words before he spoke them.

Kimberley found her eyes riveted to his. He seemed to be waiting. But he had the floor!

'But—but you had something to—add?' she questioned, fixed by the steady look of him, the look that said he did have something to add, but that he expected her reaction might be fairly explosive. She searched in her mind for what it could be. She thought he had told her the worst about Bramcote. Surely he didn't have anything to add that could possibly be worse? 'What— is it?' she asked, and was nowhere near to suspecting what it was, when after another steady look at her, he said quietly:

'I will restore Bramcote, Kimberley, and see that it's maintained as it should be, on one condition.'

'Condition?' Her mind scattered in all directions, a certainty in her that she wasn't going to like it, whatever it was. 'Er——' she began, her tongue coming out to moisten suddenly dry lips, 'what condition, Slade?'

'That you,' he said slowly, enunciating every word, 'sell me the place.'

CHAPTER SEVEN

FOR an age after Slade had dropped out his condition for maintaining her home, Kimberley did not move, but just sat and stared dumbfounded. So unexpected had his words been that for long moments she couldn't believe he had actually said what he had.

But as he looked back, unflinching, just as though he could see nothing so world-shaking in what he had said, his words spoken clearly, Kimberley knew she had not misheard him.

And as that realisation burst in, she was reacting violently, was out of her chair, her eyes showing the antipathy with which she received his suggestion.

'Sell Bramcote to you?' came scorching from her, the very idea utterly preposterous. 'Never! No, never!'

In contrast to her outrage, Slade remained calm, was cool where she was ready to burst into flames. 'What have you against it?' he asked, his hands relaxed on the arms of his chair, entirely unmoved that she was reeling from what he had said.

'You have the nerve to ask?' flew from her. 'I have everything against it! It's unthinkable! I wouldn't dream of parting with Bramcote, as you very well know.'

'But you wouldn't be parting with it,' he said, his tone reasonable, as unhurriedly he left his chair and came over to her. 'You would still be living here,' he pointed out, and taking hold of her arm, this time instead of snarling at her to sit down, gently he led her back to her chair.

A numbness was coming to Kimberley now the initial shock was subsiding. She sat making no attempt to

stir, but watched while Slade waited to see she was
staying put. Then she saw him go back to his own
chair, before, with logic she didn't want to hear, he
pointed out:

'If something isn't done about the house very soon,
I'm afraid you won't have a house at all.'

'It's—not as bad as that,' she said, her voice choky,
as she wondered, was it? If the roof wasn't put right, if
the ceilings caved in, if the plaster started to perish on
the other walls . . . She shut her mind off before she
got as far as plumbing and electric wiring.

'Be sensible, Kim,' he urged, seeing from her face
that there was no need to stress the condition the house
was in. 'You can have anyone you like to value it.'

'To hear you talk it isn't worth very much,' she
muttered.

'I didn't say that. Land is expensive. You have an
orchard and fine lawns.' Well, it was something that
he found anything to admire about the place, she
thought mutinously. 'I'll pay the full price without
quibbling,' he went on. 'You would have money in
your pocket and still have your home.'

'I'm not interested in money,' she said, throwing
him a malignant look.

'I know you're not,' he agreed, a half smile coming
her way, 'but it would be security for you.'

She knew what that half smile meant, just as she
knew what his real meaning was. What he was really
saying was that when he left her, as he was sure to,
then she would have no need to worry about her
financial security. As if that had ever bothered her!
She wasn't quite sure why it should bother Slade
either that she come out of this marriage financially
better off—though she thought it might probably
have something to do with him being shaken on dis-
covering the small amount, by comparison, she had
to live on.

'What good would financial security be if I didn't

have Bramcote?' she challenged. And following her line of thought, 'You could divorce me any time you wanted, tell me to leave.'

She saw straight away that she had annoyed him, saw the cool look leave, his mouth harden. But why he should take offence at her bringing out what she saw to be the truth, be offended at her suggesting that once he had grown fed up with her he would dump her and Bramcote, she couldn't think.

'You would have another sort of security if you were a proper wife,' he told her tautly, his eyes glinting. 'If you were a proper wife I wouldn't have any grounds for divorcing you, would I?'

'If I . . .' Her throat dried as she tried to deny what he was saying. 'You don't mean . . .'

He shrugged, his face stern. 'I'm a normal man. I have a man's normal—appetite.'

His meaning couldn't be denied. Inwardly Kimberley shrank away as it registered that Slade, for all, apart from that first night, he had made no demands on her, was clearly telling her that his desire for her body, the reason he had married her, had never waned. She felt suffocated at the cold way he was telling her that she had a way of securing Bramcote. That way was to allow him to possess her!

'That's disgusting,' she cried. 'Blackmail!' His eyes narrowed at the word, but he neither agreed nor disagreed. 'It's—it's like selling myself for the house,' she said hoarsely.

The coldness left him, and she saw him smile that smile she didn't like. 'It is, isn't it?' he said pleasantly. Then his tone toughening. 'Come now, Kimberley, didn't you believe that was what you'd done when you married me?'

'I . . .' She stopped, and threw him a look of dislike that he had her there. And he knew he had, the swine. 'I didn't think about that side of it,' she said lamely, hating him afresh that he had her on the defensive.

But she had come a long way from the girl who for many months had been untouched by life, the girl whose only emotion had been that of grief, first at David's rejection of her, then at her father's passing. And anger was stirring that he had backed her into a corner. Kimberley came out fighting.

'Can't you satiate your *normal appetite* elsewhere?' she fired. And as memory returned of the hours he had spent away from Amberton yesterday, along with his reputation, she frowned. 'Or have you already?'

Her answer was a bland smile she didn't care for. She didn't like either the look about him that said she had given him a good idea.

He rose to his feet, her question still unanswered. 'I think I'll go to bed. I want to leave early for London in the morning.' And while she sat there thinking she knew very well what he was going to London for, he said, 'Think about what I've said, Kimberley,' and left her.

After a restless night, Kimberley got up the next morning to find Slade had already gone. She checked his room, saw it was neat and tidy, his bed made, and closed the door on his room, but not on him.

He was in her mind a great deal during that day. The first reminder of him was when before ten the deep-freeze he had ordered was delivered and installed. Oh, how she wished she could say a permanent goodbye to him and his deep-freeze, she thought, niggled to find herself wondering if even now he had his arms round some female he kept around for such occasions.

It was a better day, the sun was coming out. But the garden was still too wet for her to go out and get lost in gardening, so she set about giving the house another clean. She was disgruntled again when about five she began to wonder what time Slade would be back, and if he would be hungry when he came in.

She didn't want to cook for him, but since she might as well cook something for herself, it wouldn't hurt to make enough for two.

At seven o'clock she had a delicious-smelling steak and kidney pie in the oven. There was no sign of Slade when half an hour later she put potatoes on to boil. They had been boiling for ten minutes when the phone rang.

'Where are you?' she asked when she heard Slade's voice. If he hadn't started back yet her lovely steak and kidney would be dried up.

'London.'

'What time will you be back?' Kimberley asked. Then as the dreadful thought occurred to her that he might think she was eager for his return, hurriedly she explained, 'I've made a steak and kidney pie for dinner, and it will be ruined if you don't get here soon.'

'You can eat my share,' he told her carelessly. 'I'm ringing to say I won't be back tonight.'

'You're not coming home!' It was something she hadn't thought of, which was odd, because when he had gone to London the day before yesterday she had thought, hoped, for nothing better than that he would stay there.

'I'm—er—tied up,' said Slade blithely. And, showing just how unconcerned he was, 'Did the freezer arrive, by the way?'

'The potatoes are boiling over,' she lied, and slammed the phone down.

She regretted the impulse as soon as the phone was back in its cradle. Slade would know she was mad at him since as there was no phone in the kitchen it was impossible for her to see how the potatoes were faring. Oh, how she hated that man!

But it was when she was in bed that night, wanting to sleep, but sleep a million miles away, that Kimberley

realised she did not hate Slade. Not that she felt anything else in particular for him either, she decided
quickly. But—she remembered how he had made her
smile more than once—he wasn't so unbearable to have
around. And already since knowing him she had started
to gain some of the weight she had lost.

She turned over in her bed, wishing she could
sleep. She wasn't missing him, she was sure about that.
She scoffed at the mere idea. No, she definitely wasn't
missing him, any more than he was missing her.

That brought to mind thoughts of him so much not
missing her that he was probably at this very moment
tucked up in bed, and with his reputation, not alone
either. And she was back to hating him again—until
she remembered he had thought of her once since he
had left the house, even if his phone call had been so
offhand he needn't have bothered.

The next day the weather was a decided improve-
ment, and since the house was as clean as a new pin,
Kimberley spent most of it outside weeding the garden
paths. The frozen food Slade had ordered arrived late
in the afternoon, taking her indoors to stay. She had
enough food in for a siege, she thought, but it was
staying where it was. If Slade wanted a meal when he
came home tonight—if he came home tonight, she qualified—then he could get it himself.

Around seven she made herself an egg on toast, and
sat eating it in the kitchen, her ears attuned without
her being conscious of it for the sound of his car.

At ten o'clock she was sick and tired of waiting for
him to appear, and went to bed not very happy at all
that he hadn't even had the decency that evening to so
much as pick up a phone to tell her he wouldn't be
back. So much for him offering to buy Bramcote! Well,
he could jolly well come and collect his three suitcases—and his perishing freezer! She wanted nothing
of him or his in her house—falling down as it might
be.

She hadn't been in bed long when in the silence of the night she heard the sound of a car. She heard footsteps outside, but stayed where she was, determined to be asleep when Slade crossed her room to go to his bed.

But the sound of the front door bell sent the memory rushing in that she had locked up and that Slade hadn't got a key, and forced her out of bed and into her dressing gown, her face stormy as she opened the front door.

'So good of you to come home at all,' she fired, and was staggered to hear her voice sounding just like the shrew he had said he had married. She spun round from the dark-suited figure of Slade, and bolted back to her bed.

She heard his footsteps coming along the landing, and though appalled by what she had done, was still angry enough that he could treat her house as though it was some lodging house, she was unrepentant.

'Miss me?' Slade enquired, entering her room and coming to stand by the bed where she sat glowering at him.

'Pardon me if I don't collapse at your sense of humour,' she retorted acidly.

Without comment he turned, opening the dressing room door, shrugging out of his coat and flinging it to his bed, his tie following it. So that was it, Kimberley thought; a sardonic 'Miss me?' was all she was going to get for him being away tomcatting for nearly two whole days.

On the point of sliding down the bed, having no idea why she should be getting uptight since she didn't care a button what Slade Darville, her husband, did, she saw he had turned, his eyes taking in her mutinous face. And before she could get down the bed and close her eyes he had come from his room, stood for a second looking down at her, and then without so much as a by your leave, he was sitting down on the coverlet and murmuring:

'What a sensitive creature you are, Kimberley!'

She hadn't been expecting him to say anything like that, hadn't expected to hear that kind note in his voice. It stopped her mutinous thoughts dead and had her defending that sensitivity he had somehow seen.

'I—haven't inherited my mother's highly strung nature,' she said, not looking at him.

He took hold of her hand, his touch warm and calming. The gentleness of his touch made her allow him to keep hold of her hand, when had it not been so she would have snatched it back in no uncertain fashion.

'No, I don't think you have,' he said softly. 'But from somewhere you've inherited a great sensitivity that makes you very vulnerable.'

Her eyes flicked to his. She saw a gentleness there too that matched the touch of him as lightly his other hand came to stroke her arm. She wanted to look away, but felt mesmerised by the dark blue eyes that held hers.

'I shall have to give you the spare key,' she said huskily, no acid in her now.

'That would be an idea,' said Slade. Then, 'I want to kiss you before I go to bed.'

Vaguely Kimberley thought Slade's manner verged on being seductive. But she gave no mind then to the thoughts that had been in her head about him being in London with some other woman. All that fixed in her mind was that he had said 'before I go to bed' and that must mean he had no intention of making her bed his bed.

'Y-you've kissed me goodnight before,' she said, and remembered she had found his kisses quite pleasurable—that one time.

It was all the invitation he needed—though it was without haste that he let go of her hand and gently gathered her into his arms. And then he did not kiss her straight away, but held her there in the circle of his strong arms, looking down at her so that the ridiculous idea popped into her head that whether she had missed him or not, Slade had missed her.

Her heart was beating rapidly when at last his head came down and he laid gentle lips on hers. She made no attempt to kiss him back, but found she would not have objected had his mouth rested on hers a little longer than the brief moment it had.

'G-goodnight,' she stammered, when, still holding her, he pulled back to look into her eyes.

'Aren't you going to tell me what you've been doing while I've been away?' he enquired softly, making no move to let her go.

It came to her then that it would be more to the point to ask him what he had been doing while he was away. But as his mouth came over hers a second time, the question went from her. His mouth was warm, teasing, and this time it stayed over hers a couple of seconds longer, drawing away the moment he felt her minute response.

Kimberley knew herself disappointed, and tried hard to remember what his question had been. 'I—er—did some housework yesterday,' she said, and her heart-beats quickened when Slade looked warmly at her, then unhurriedly moved her until she was lying back against the pillows, the upper part of his body covering hers as again he kissed her.

A thrill of excitement quivered in her, and her arms went round him, the heat of his body through his thin shirt making her fully aware she was holding on to a full-blooded male.

'And what did you do today?' Slade enquired, his mouth leaving hers to transfer to her shoulder.

'Today,' said Kimberley, having difficulty to remember it was Thursday without the added complication of trying to remember what she had done, 'I—er—d-did some gardening.'

His lips were tormenting her, whispering in light

kisses along her throat to where the swell of her breasts began. 'The ground was dry enough for you to garden?' he asked softly, raising his head to look deep into her eyes.

She tried to avoid his look, knew her face was flushed. Then before she could reply, she felt his mouth capture hers, his kiss deepening, having her responding, clutching on to him.

'Yes,' she said, her voice hushed, when his lips left hers and he looked deep into her eyes again.

'Yes?' he said, the glow in his eyes telling her he had misinterpreted the word.

Not sure that she hadn't wanted him to misinterpret it, Kimberley struggled for sanity. 'I mean, yes, the—er—ground was d-dry enough for me to do some gardening,' she gulped, and saw him smile.

'You're beautiful, Kim,' he breathed, and kissed her again, his hands caressing her. They were still caressing her when he asked, 'Have you seen anyone since I left, had any visitors?'

'Er—no,' she said, trembling slightly when his eyes fixed to hers he removed the strap of her nightdress and pulled it down to expose her breast. 'I—er—that is,' she said, her voice wobbly for all he was looking at her and not at what his fingers had exposed, 'the—er—men delivered the deep-freeze yesterday.' She had told him that, she thought, or had she? She could barcly remember that phone call as with his eyes still holding hers, his hand caressed over her shoulder and down to capture her breast.

Her eyes widened at his touch, but more from the wanton feeling he was arousing in her than from the thought of where all this was leading.

'It's all right my, darling,' Slade said, reading from her look that she wasn't certain about anything any more.

He kissed her then, a gentle kiss, then was transferring his mouth to her breast, had her tensing that she

was in a no-man's-land when she felt moistness from
the inside of his mouth erecting the peak of her breast.

'Slade,' she said shakily. Then he was lying beside
her, the covers taken from her as he pressed the length
of his body against hers. She felt his need for her, felt
that same need in her for him, and was trembling from
the emotion of it.

'Ssh,' he soothed. 'It will be all right for you, my
dear.'

But her trembling, which had only taken a real hold
when he had left talking of unrelated matters to get
closer to her, wouldn't stop. Whether Slade too
realised this, she had no idea, but he began again to
talk gently to her, kissing her again and again in between the soothing comfort of his voice as he said anything that came into his head.

Her trembling eased, she felt herself on fire for him
as, his shirt disposed of, she felt his hair-roughened
chest press against her naked breasts. She felt the
caress of a kiss feather her ear as, still speaking softly,
Slade asked her had she thought any more about selling
the house to him.

And it was at that point, his words impinging on her
need for him, that Kimberley had to fight with all she
had against that need, fight against the longing he had
aroused.

From the beginning she hadn't played fair with him.
How now, when he had said he would buy the house
and repair it, could she secure for herself the knowledge that as his 'proper wife' she would still have
Bramcote? How could she so willingly consummate
their marriage—leave him powerless to divorce her—
when as yet she had made no decision to sell the house
to him? Wouldn't that be like cheating again?

His mouth was about to take hers once more, passion
increasing as words were left behind, when Kimberley
had to make her voice heard, and, 'Don't!' ripped from
her.

It stayed him. But she didn't dare to see the look in his eyes. She guessed he was more aroused now than he had been that time before when he had torn her nightdress. She was desperately afraid she had left it too late and that tearing her nightdress would be mild in comparison with what she had let herself in for now. She pushed away from him, too much aware of her naked upper half as she sat up, turning her back to him.

She heard him move, felt the electric silence coming from him, but was afraid to turn, to look at him, to see his anger.

'Bennet?'

The word was clipped. It was all he said. That was all he was asking, she saw. He was asking had thoughts of David penetrated between the giving and taking that had been theirs.

She shook her head, expecting any moment to feel aggressively rough hands on her shoulders hauling her on to her back where the word 'Don't' would make not the slightest difference. Then, with amazement, she heard Slade's voice, relatively mildly:

'What, then?'

'I—haven't come to a decision about the house yet,' she said, feeling dreadfully cold suddenly, where seconds before she had felt on fire.

But she knew she had to go on, had to convince him before that glimmer of mildness deserted him. 'You offered me security in return for . . .' God, how awful that sounded! Her blood turned to ice. But she made herself go on, gritting her teeth as she told him, 'I can't g-give myself to you and—and by so doing take that security you offered in—r-return for my body— when I haven't yet made up my mind to sell Bramcote to you.'

She knew then, as a silence stretched behind her, that Slade was thinking her idiotic. She wondered herself how clear her thinking was, since she had thought only of securing Bramcote when she had married him, but accepted that the effect of his lovemaking was enough to have her muddle-headed.

She braced herself to feel hard hands bearing down on her, then was fighting against fresh confusion when at last his voice reached her, his voice kind, gentle, the way it had been all through their lovemaking.

'Will you be all right if I leave you?' he asked. 'You haven't any tablets, remember.'

Kimberley hadn't given thought to needing a tranquilliser, but she knew suddenly that she could cope without them. Though at the same time she realised, had she been going to need one at all, it would only be because she was shattered at the incredible knowledge that Slade didn't look as if he was going to cut up rough. She took a gulp of air.

'I'll be all right,' she said.

She was never so staggered as when Slade stayed only long enough to drop a light kiss on her bare shoulder, just as if he found her naked back irresistible, then went quickly to his room and quietly closed the door.

Kimberley sat there for long, long minutes after that door had closed. Thoughts of the mighty control Slade must have on himself threatened to sink her. He had wanted her, she had no doubt about that. His need for her had been urgent, she had felt that too. Yet he had somehow managed to control that conquering male aggression in him, had got up from the bed and left her when she had explained her reasons. He had even had the thoughtfulness to ask if she would be all right!

She lay down in bed, the fresh thought coming that maybe the reason he had been able to leave her without that aggression showing was because his need for a woman's body had been slaked in London. She did not like the thought.

Then she had to wonder at herself—the desire Slade had been able to awaken in her. How she had been ready to give herself to him even when she was fairly convinced he had been having a high old time in London.

Her body chemistry had a lot to answer for, she thought, then promptly left thoughts of her own traitorous body as she recalled that he had thought it had been thoughts of David coming to her that had had her calling 'Don't!'

And she was further staggered then to realise that since her broken engagement, when she had been eaten up with thoughts of her ex-fiancé, for the past two days, she had not thought of David—not once.

CHAPTER EIGHT

AT dawn Kimberley awoke, to be bombarded with memories of what had so nearly happened between her and Slade the night before. What on earth had come over her that the voice of protest had been nowhere to be heard? She had been ready to give herself to him right until up to the time he had questioned whether she had come to any decision about selling Bramcote!

With no one there to see, hot colour flooded her face as she recalled the way his bare chest had been pressed against her naked breasts.

Wanting to rid herself of all memory of the previous night, of how pliant she had been in his arms, Kimberley got rapidly out of her bed. She was washed and dressed in record time, and was sitting in the kitchen to find her memories had followed her, that she couldn't escape them so easily.

Slade had once told her it wouldn't be rape if ever he took her, and now she could believe him. She had been as mad as hell with him for treating her home like a lodging house, coming to Bramcote when he had left off his activities in London. But in a very short space of time he had turned her from the shrewish woman who had opened the door to him into a clinging woman who had soon forgotten any thoughts she had had that she wasn't the first woman he had had in his arms that day.

Well, it mustn't be allowed to happen again, she resolved. For her own self-respect she had to keep him away from her. She now knew that he could overcome her resistance to him, so she had, for her own peace of mind, to keep away from him.

For going on two hours Kimberley sat in her kitchen

132

pondering on the unpleasant thought that to the Slade Darvilles of this world, another woman succumbing to their sexual prowess was no more than they expected.

She left her chair and went to make a pot of tea, saw her hands were shaking, and knew just why. She was dreading having to face Slade again. Her insides turned over at just the very thought. Oh, why didn't he get up so she could get that first meeting over with and then be able to put that scene, which she still found stupefying to remember had ended with him leaving her without getting angry, behind her?

Kimberley poured herself a cup of tea, her mind returning to the thought she had had last night. The thought that Slade hadn't turned nasty as she had expected, and that the reason he hadn't was plain to see. The edge had been taken off his appetite before he had driven his car in the direction of the village of Amberton.

This is crazy, she thought, knowing her brain wouldn't give her a moment's rest from the subject that had filled it for the past few hours, until Slade appeared, that first meeting over.

In a mood of—well, she wasn't sitting around waiting all day for him to come out of his exhausted (and she knew why) slumber, Kimberley stood up, collected a tray, and poured tea into a second cup.

She was in her bedroom, the closed dressing room door facing her before she got cold feet. Then knowing the alternative was to go back downstairs and have her brain chasing after that same theme that had already been done to death, she went forward.

Her brief knock on the door that separated the two rooms had disturbed him. He opened his eyes as she went in, then rolled from his back on to his side, propping himself up on one elbow, his eyes following her as she moved to the small bedside table and transferred the cup and saucer from the tray.

Her colour was high—she knew it was, and was

thankful Slade couldn't see the turmoil going on inside her at the sight of the darker hair on his chest, his chest that had been . . .

He caught hold of her wrist staying her when, her eyes averted, she would have left him without comment. 'This is just like being at home, having morning tea brought to me,' he remarked softly.

'It's time you got up,' she told him sourly.

Then she saw he was the type who woke up in a disgustingly sunny humour, as, not taking offence, even when she snatched her wrist out of his hold, he asked equally:

'Have you got a good morning kiss for me?'

Tight-lipped, Kimberley looked at his tormenting face and met his eyes without flinching, although her cheeks were pink.

'Is that what you received in London yesterday morning—a good morning kiss?'

She wished she had tipped the tea all over him when, instead of him being stung by her remark as she hoped, his face creased into a wicked grin as he told her:

'The divorce, my darling, is going to be my prerogative.' And with a whole cartload of charm, 'Am I likely, do you think, to admit to anything that will give you an ace?'

Kimberley slammed out, wishing heartily that she had forgotten to put the two spoons of sugar he liked in his tea. Had that wicked look in his eye come from remembrance of the sweetness of the female he had awakened with yesterday? Thank God she hadn't gone the same way; although it had been a near thing.

The morning mail had been delivered by the time Slade joined her, tears that had been a stranger to her these past few days catching her at the unexpectedness of seeing a couple of bills addressed to her father.

'Have you had breakfast?' Slade addressed her bent head as she swallowed back sad tears.

'I don't want any,' she said quietly.

She heard him move, come to the side of her. 'What have you got there?'

'Just a couple of bills,' she said, and left her sad thoughts behind as without more ado he took the phone and electricity bills out of her hands and calmly told her:

'I'll settle these.' And just as though by his lofty statement he would pay for services he hadn't used, the matter was finished with, 'Have we any bacon?'

'You won't settle them!' she fired, her eyes still moist, sparking dangerously.

Slade looked back at her and she saw then as his expression became chiselled, that the aggression that hadn't surfaced last night was now looking for an outlet.

'I could have taken you last night,' he told her gratingly, bringing out into the open a subject she had no intention of discussing, 'but I didn't. Don't try and get away with murder today, Kimberley. You just might push me too far.'

She wanted to tell him he wasn't going to browbeat her, plus a hundred other things she could think of. But the look on his face told her he meant it when he had said she just might push him too far. And suddenly she was too afraid what his retribution might be, and had nothing to come back with when, after giving her ample time, Slade turned from her, pushing the bills into his pocket.

Well, he could cook his own breakfast, she thought, and hoped he burnt his bacon, as she went upstairs to make her bed and tidy up.

She stayed upstairs for a long time. Then she saw from her bedroom window that Slade had got the antiquated lawnmower out of the shed. She watched while he made a short attempt to mow one lawn, then saw him give it up. She could have told him the mower was on its last legs.

The next time she peeped out she saw he was having

a go at servicing the mower. So he didn't want her
company either, she thought, having decided a few
hours ago to go into hiding if he yelled up the stairs
for her to come down and eat breakfast.

He hadn't called her down and demanded she eat, so
she gathered from that he was fed up with her and
didn't care a damn if she did lose those few pounds
she had put on.

It was half past eleven when she went down to make
herself a cup of coffee. He had already had tea in bed,
and she didn't want to make him a cup of coffee. But
her own coffee was steaming in its beaker, a feeling of
being mean came over her.

She went to the kitchen door, opened it, called,
'Coffee!' and closed it again. If he hadn't heard then
she had made the effort, hadn't she?

Slade came in, washing his hands at the sink. But
Kimberley was finding her coffee of the utmost interest.

'Still sulking?' came the cool enquiry.

Hot words rose, but she bit them back. 'You bring
out the best in me,' she said sweetly.

'I enjoyed it too,' he said, mockery there, so she
knew just exactly what he was talking about.

'Have you got the mower to work yet?' she enquired,
playing dumb, and heard him laugh.

She didn't laugh with him. But it was as though
hearing him laugh had banished her blues. She felt a
smile in her at any rate, which was a pleasing change
from feeling down, the way she had all morning, as
Slade then asked how long she had had the mower and
they discussed its few merits.

Kimberley was rinsing out the mugs they had used
when she heard the mower start up, and glancing
through the window, she saw Slade push it on to the
lawn—and actually caught herself singing softly as she
investigated the larder deciding what to have for lunch.
Then she stopped singing as it came to her that she

would have to get down to thinking what she was going to do about her lovely home. She still thought of it as lovely even though to hear Slade talk it needing something doing to it before too long.

By the time lunch was ready she had swung this way and that, and was still no nearer to knowing what she should do.

It came to her consciousness that she hadn't heard the mower for some ten minutes now. That must mean it had either packed up, or that Slade had finished. She went to the door to tell him lunch would soon be ready, then stopped on the threshold. He was at the far end of the garden, his hand resting on the mower, having cut the engine as he passed the time of day with old Sammy.

David would never have done that, she found herself thinking. He would never have cut the noisy engine to stop and have a few words with the old boy. Now wasn't it nice of Slade to do that? she thought, and was taken aback by the thought that came from nowhere; that Slade was a much nicer person than David.

Kimberley was back in her kitchen when the door opened and Slade came in, 'Something smells good,' he remarked as he went to the sink. 'I thought it might be nosebag time when I saw you come to the door.'

He turned from the sink, taking up the towel to dry his hands, his action stopping momentarily as he looked her way and saw her pale face.

'Something wrong?' he asked at once.

She shook her head. How could she tell him, when she didn't believe it herself, that she had compared him with David and had actually seen him in a more favourable light!

'Don't bottle it up, Kim,' Slade said, discarding the towel and coming over to take hold of her by the shoulders. 'Something *is* worrying you. Is it the house?'

About to shake her head again, Kimberley looked

up into his sincere blue eyes. And she knew in that instant that in the matter of Bramcote, if nothing else, she could trust him.

'About the house, Slade,' she said, and seizing on a moment of courage, 'w-will—would you buy it from me?'

For nerve-racking seconds, as he looked sternly at her without answering, she thought he had changed his mind. And she knew panic that if he wouldn't do as he had said, she just didn't know what she was going to do.

'I've said I will,' he said at long last, but paused, his look severe still as he asked what she had fogotten. 'I will keep my word, Kimberley, as I always intended, but how about you?'

Her brow puckered. 'What about me?'

'More specifically—what about the normal marriage we spoke of?'

'Oh,' she said. Bramcote, losing title to it to the front of her mind—she had forgotten that part of the deal. But she remembered then. Remembered too the thoughts that had come unceasingly to her early that morning that her own self-respect demanded she should not be just some village girl he had tucked away for when he got bored with the sophisticated women he knew in London.

She moved out of his hold, and he let her go. She nibbled at her bottom lip, knowing he was being fair. She saw it was to her advantage to close that loophole that gave him cause to divorce her before February, when she could lose Bramcote anyway. But still she could not give him her word that she would be his.

'I'm—I'm not ready yet, Slade,' she stammered, and, facing him, 'I—need time to—to adjust.'

She saw then from the slight narrowing of his eyes that he was thinking she had seemed to be adjusting more than well last night. That the only reason then that she hadn't given in completely, so she had said, was because she hadn't made up her mind about the very subject they were discussing.

And then she felt a definite liking for him when, although it was clear what he was thinking, Slade forbore to say any of it.

But what he did say had her feeling winded that she didn't know the answer, when point blank he asked:

'Are you still in love with David Bennet?'

The very positive answer of 'yes' was ready on her tongue before she thought about it. But when she went to say it, the word wouldn't leave her. For one crazy moment her world spun round. A week ago there had been no doubt in her mind. But—she didn't know any longer!

She was gasping, not believing she could be so unsure. 'I—don't know,' she choked. 'I—honestly don't know.'

She saw Slade smile the moment before he came and half pushed, half helped her down into a chair. 'Rocked you, has it?' he said, not unkindly. 'Sit there and get your breath while I take whatever smells as though it's got a nice burnt crust out of the oven.'

He was treating her like an invalid. And indeed her legs did feel shaky. But she could manage herself to rescue their meal. She got up from the chair he had pushed her into and reached for an oven cloth at the same time as he was reaching for the thick towel that would have served the same purpose.

Over lunch Slade asked her the name of her solicitor and where he could be found. 'Charles Forester,' she told him. 'He has offices in Thaxly.' And, not sure why he wanted the information, she asked, 'Why?'

'Because it's in your interests that your legal adviser is in on the sale of Bramcote from the very beginning.'

'You know I can't . . .'

'Come to me yet?' he queried, saving her the embarrassment of having to go over again what she had told him in the kitchen. He smiled with some charm, his eyes holding hers deliberately as he said softly, 'I can wait.' Then he went on swiftly to tell her her lawyer would probably be able to tell her the best man to value the property, ending with, 'We'll go and see him this afternoon—do you have his number?'

As Slade had once told her, he didn't hang about once a decision had been made. He was taking her breath away with the speed he intended to move. But even so, he could have no idea that the pace of life in this part of the world was a whole lot slower than in the London he was more used to.

'It might be next week before you can get an appointment to see Mr Forester,' she thought she'd better warn him.

Her answer was a benign smile. Clearly he didn't share her doubts. 'He'll see us today,' he said confidently. 'I want to be in my office for nine on Monday.'

So he was starting back to work next week, Kimberley mused, as taking her with him to the phone Slade dialled the number she had given him, and was charming his way past Charles Forester's gorgon of a secretary and speaking to the man himself.

Kimberley still hadn't recovered when with Slade she set about washing up before they left to keep the appointment he had made for them in Thaxly for three that afternoon. Without fuss he had told Charles Forester that his client Miss Kimberley Adams was now his wife, and while Mr Forester was getting over that, told him in a voice that would entertain no refusal that he would like to see him that afternoon to discuss the disposal of the property she was due to inherit. What Mr Forester made of that she didn't know, though she thought maybe the way Slade had phrased it had had the effect of making him want to get in there quick before she sold something that wasn't yet legally hers.

'Slade,' she said slowly, sitting in the car beside him on the way into Thaxly. He took his eyes briefly from the road at the hesitancy in her voice.

'Problem?' he prompted.

'It's only just occurred to me, but can I sell Bramcote to you before the six months is up?'

From his answer she gleaned Slade had not overlooked that point. 'With or without my legal people looking at your father's will for a loophole, I doubt it,' he said easily, his eyes steady on the road in front, going on to show her his brain cogs had very little chance of going rusty. 'What I have in mind is for a legally binding contract to be drawn up so that on the date you're due to inherit, the house becomes mine.'

'Can you do that?'

'We'll let the legal boys work out the whys and wherefores,' he said, turning to give her a smile of some charm. 'Don't worry your head about it. Once Bramcote has been valued and the contract I spoke of signed, the sale price will be paid over to you, we can get the builders in.'

He had it all cut and dried, it seemed. The money was of no importance to her and she had no idea how long all this would take, but it was a certainty that the roof wouldn't wait until February. She could only hope Mr Forester would raise no objection to what was planned.

Promptly at three they were shown in to see the elderly man who had handled her father's business for years. Feeling nervous, Kimberley introduced the two men, saw them sizing each other up, Mr Forester commenting as he invited both of them to take a seat that he hadn't known she was due to be married the last time she had visited him.

'You'll want to see this, of course,' said Slade, extracting what Kimberley saw was their marriage certificate, and passing it over with the pleasantly voiced, 'We did discuss waiting a respectful amount of time, but with my wife's father leaving the will he did, and knowing how fond Kimberley is of her home, it seemed to us he was anxious that we marry without delay.'

'Er—quite so,' nodded Mr Forester.

'It's about the property we've come to see you, isn't it, darling?' Slade added, turning to send a lingering smile her way before turning his attention back to the solicitor. Then concisely he outlined what he wanted to do.

'I don't know,' said Mr Forester ponderously. 'There may be problems with a mortgage in a case like this.'

But when Slade told him he wouldn't be requiring a mortgage, going on to tell him the name of a well-known firm of solicitors who would be contacting him on his behalf, Kimberley saw any doubt in Mr Forester's lined face start to fade.

By the time they left fifteen minutes later, Mr Forester had asked what work Slade did, discovered he knew his firm, and if anything was beginning to look as though he thought Kimberley had done very well for herself indeed. But she had grown far from happy with the solicitor's attitude.

'I didn't marry you for your money,' she muttered when they reached the street—and only realised she was on the verge of being a crosspatch when she heard Slade laugh, and tease:

'You should have told him you loved me.'

'Get you!' she said, but had to smile herself.

'What we want now is a reputable builder,' said Slade. 'Any idea who's the best?'

'I don't think your solicitor would want you to have the repairs done before I've signed that contract,' Kimberley said thoughtfully, guessing that was what he had in mind—then had to stop when Slade did since he had hold of her arm.

'You're a darling,' he said out of the blue, his eyes warm on her face.

'What did I do?' she asked, mystified that he should

halt her in the middle of the High Street to tell her that.

Right there he bent down and kissed the tip of her nose, reminding her of their wedding day when in this same street she had done something similar.

'Take back all I ever said about you being selfish. I'm supposed to be looking after your interests, not the other way about,' he said. Then he was marching her forward again, as he went on. 'Since only the best builders are good enough to have a go at Bramcote,' he said, which made her spirits rise, 'if I'm any judge they're going to have a full order book. I doubt if we shall be able to get them started before we've both signed on the dotted line.'

It was just as well Slade had a nose for those sort of things, Kimberley thought when some time later they were on their way back to Amberton. She didn't know one builder from another, but Slade had soon ferreted out the offices of a first class firm. His only regret was that because he would be working on Monday, he wouldn't be there to show their representative, when he came, what in his opinion needed doing.

Her mind was full of the never-ending list of things Slade had said he wanted the estimator to look at when he arrived. And it wasn't just repairs he wanted attending to either. Though Kimberley wasn't left to feel so much that Bramcote was being taken out of her hands completely, when Slade included her in the talk of turning one of the bedrooms that had been used more as a junk room than anything else into a super de luxe bathroom.

'Bramcote will still be yours, Kim,' Slade said suddenly, quietly, as he drove along, just as though he thought she was feeling down about it.

'I hadn't realised so much needed doing to, to make it habitable,' she said back.

'You'll like it when it's finished, I promise you,' he replied gravely, then went on to show that his mind worked far in advance of hers. 'Which leads me to mention,' he said, as if considering every word, 'that you'll have to come and stay with me in London for a short time while the builders are in.'

'Stay with you? Leave Bramcote?' The idea horrified her and it showed in her voice. She half expected Slade to get short with her, and she did hear sarcasm there when he said:

'When you decide which is the lesser of the two evils let me know.' Then he was biting down whatever he was feeling, as he went on reasonably, 'Your own common sense will tell you you can't stay at Bramcote when the roof comes off.'

Did he have to be so right? She swallowed down her irritation the way he had done. 'Shouldn't I stay around to supervise? I could stay at the Rose and Crown.'

'We can come down each weekend,' Slade's voice overrode hers, causing Kimberley to wonder just how long the building work was going to take. Then she wasn't thinking about the builders at all when Slade told her evenly, 'And to save you from getting in a stew wondering if you're going to have to share a bed with me, I'll tell you now that if things haven't resolved themselves between us by then,' he broke off, and she held her breath, 'then I do have a spare room you can retire chastely to until they do.'

'You think of everything!' She tried for sweet sarcasm. She wasn't liking Slade Darville and his I-dotting, T-crossing bluntness very much at that moment.

She was on edge with him after that, fears growing as time for bed came that night, that for all he had said to the contrary, tonight might see a repeat performance of last night when he had very nearly seduced her. It would have helped if he had made some attempt to tease her out of the quiet mood that had fallen on her on that homeward journey from Thaxly, but he hadn't, and she wished mightily that she knew what he was thinking. She had caught him looking at her several times, his look slanting off her when he had seen her catching him at it.

Oh, how she wished he didn't have to come through her room to get to his own! Unconsciously she sighed, then jumped startled at the way that, hearing her sigh, Slade impatiently threw down the paper he was reading.

'I'm going to—to bed,' burst from her before he could speak.

Slade rose when she rose, doing nothing for her nervousness of him when he came and stood in front of her, stopping her from going anywhere.

His hand came beneath her chin, forcing her head up when she didn't want to look at him. His expression grim when he felt her tremble.

'I've left you alone with your thoughts,' he stated baldly, 'because I realise a lot has happened for you today. I thought you needed time with your own thoughts, time to come to terms with it all. I've been honest with you about the house and more gratified than you can know at the trust you've shown in me over it.' Dumbly Kimberley stared at him. She had never seen his face so stern as he continued, 'I told you about having to move to my London home because it would have come to you anyway that you couldn't stay here, and I wanted to save you worry about where you would go. For the same reason, Kimberley, to save you from worrying, I've told you—if need be—you will have your own room. But this evening I've watched you going more and more into yourself. That sigh just now convinced me there's some maggot at work in your head.' His jaw jutted, letting her know her time for private thought was over. 'So out with it,' he said firmly. 'You're not going to bed tense the way you are.'

Silently Kimberley damned him and his 'stay and get everything into the open' treatment. If she thought she would have got very far she would have walked round him and out through the door. Stubbornly she looked back at him.

'I don't want to go to bed with you,' she said flatly.

'You might wait until you're asked,' came flying back at her before she could blink.

Then to her surprise she saw a smile surface from him as in the following split second he had sorted out what had been going through her head. And it was with deep sincerity that he was saying:

'I've told you I can wait. Won't you try extending that trust in me you've shown over the house?'

Bewildered suddenly, she realised what a whole lot of difference it made to her when he smiled that gentle smile at her. Tension left her almost immediately, taking with it her fears. She did trust him, she knew she did. But the words to tell him so wouldn't come.

'Try to believe me,' Slade urged, when she stayed mute in front of him, 'when I tell you that I won't come near you until you feel you can come to me willingly.'

'I—do believe you,' came struggling to the surface.

She saw his smile broaden at her words. 'Thank you,' he said simply, then, his smile going wry, 'Would you try to remember in that belief that you have a husband who's merely mortal?' and while she stared solemnly at him, he added, 'Don't make it too long before you adjust to having me for a husband.'

'I . . .' she began, lost by the charm of him.

'You could make a start right now, by kissing that same husband goodnight,' he suggested softly.

Mesmerised by him, she felt it was the most natural thing then for her to stand on tiptoe and touch her lips to his. And her trust in him was never greater than, when it seemed his arms were going to come around her, he stepped out of her path and muttered:

'Methinks you'd better get off to bed—*my* trust in

Slade Darville is standing on shaky ground at just this moment!'

Although Slade had moved fast when once he had her agreement to sell Bramcote to him, it took four weeks before the contract drawn up between the two sets of legal advisers was finally signed by them both.

And it was on the Monday following that Kimberley was in the kitchen, her tender heart going out to the victims of a motorway pile-up that had just been reported on the radio. There had been scores of cars involved, the accident happening in thick fog, so the announcer had said.

She hoped the motorway would be clear by tonight. It was the motorway Slade used to drive home. She left thoughts of the radio report to reflect how Slade had taken last Friday off to go with her to Charles Forester's office to sign everything that had to be signed.

Bramcote was virtually his now. If she wanted it back it was too late. She would probably have to pen her name once more in February when the deeds were handed over to Slade, but that enormous amount of money that had been deposited in her name in several building society accounts was proof enough that she no longer had claim to the property.

What she was going to do with all that money was beyond her. Slade had said that later, if it was her wish, he would invest some of it for her, but for the moment it wouldn't do her confidence any harm for her first to get the feeling of being a woman of means.

She wasn't quite sure what he had meant by that. She had come a long way since knowing him from that almost permanently depressed creature she had been. Looking back, she was little short of horrified at the state she had allowed herself to get into, and knew she had a tremendous amount to thank him for.

The days had turned into weeks since the night he had sworn not to come near her until she could come

willingly to him. And he had stuck to his word.
Though he still wanted her—she knew that from the
fact that when, although she had got into the habit of
giving him a brief kiss goodnight every evening, there
were some nights, more frequently this last week, when
he would back away soon after the kiss, as though the
feel of her mouth against his inflamed him.

During the afternoon Kimberley got out her cooking
utensils ready to make some meat pies to go in the
freezer. On Sunday she was moving into Slade's
London home, as the workmen were starting on
Monday, and it might be a good idea to have some
home-cooked meals ready for the weekend trips they
were to make.

At five she turned on the radio to listen to the news,
and heard that dense fog was covering the countryside,
that airfields and whole sections of some motorways
had been closed. This news had only just been broad-
cast when the phone rang. It was Slade telling her that
having had Friday off he had spent most of the day
catching up and would be late home that evening.

'There's fog everywhere,' Kimberley told him. 'I've
just heard it on the news. The section of the motorway
you use is closed.'

'I shall have to find me another route, by the look,'
said Slade. 'Though lord knows what time I shall get
home.'

'Don't come,' Kimberley said instantly. And added
quickly, 'I mean, if things are that bad, and the radio
said it was going to get worse, it could be morning
before you get here—and—and you'll have a terrible
journey again in the morning if it hasn't cleared by
then.'

She could hear the smile in his voice as he said, 'You
sound like a lady who's anxious not to hurt my feelings.'

Her own smile peeped out. 'It was you who said I
was sensitive.' Then soberly, 'Stay in London, Slade.

I shall be worried to death if you don't.'

'Worried—about me?'

Kimberley hesitated; she had grown to like Slade. 'I—er—I'm used to having you around,' she said, trying for a casual note, then heard him laugh delightedly.

'So you'll miss me if I don't come home tonight?'

'I just might,' she hedged. She heard his short laugh again, then his voice, totally serious:

'Will you be all right on your own?'

'Fine,' she answered brightly.

'I'll see you tomorrow, then.' He paused, then added intimately, 'Darling.'

Kimberley came away from the phone deep in thought. She hadn't thought the time would ever come when she would go willingly to Slade. But the very fact that he hadn't pressed or rushed her, had kept to his word, had gone a long way to weakening her resolve. Not counting the times recently his wit had had her laughing, even giggling once, she remembered.

Kimberley went back to the kitchen, but didn't straight away take up the job she had left to answer the phone. Excitement started to grow in her as she sat on one of the kitchen chairs, her hands idle.

For many minutes she didn't move. But when she did, she knew self-respect no longer came into it. She knew the period of adjustment she had told Slade she needed was over. Just as she knew the intimate 'darling' he had ended with meant that Slade too knew that his time of waiting was done.

CHAPTER NINE

KIMBERLEY opened her eyes to see sun streaming in through her bedroom window. In a flash she was out of bed and peering outside. Gone was the dense fog of yesterday. She smiled. Slade would be home tonight!

A mood of happy anticipation was in her as she showered and got ready for the day. She had had to put the bedside lamp out herself last night—and hadn't liked it. It was odd, she thought, that having truly hated Slade at one time, she should now be facing the fact that she had missed him last night.

Half way through the morning she found herself wondering if he had missed her, and a small sigh she couldn't account for escaped when she thought he probably hadn't. Not that I'm going to dwell on that, she thought, wishing she could find from somewhere that confidence in herself that had been there before David had wrecked it.

By noon David was out of her head and she was again looking forward to Slade coming home. She would make him something extra special for dinner, she thought. Perhaps he would open a bottle of his best wine to go with it, her thoughts went on.

Then all thoughts of Slade and the pleasant evening they would have were interrupted by the sound of the garden gate, of hurrying footsteps coming up the path, of someone at the door.

'Doreen!' she exclaimed, delighted to see her, remembering only then the card she had received from her saying she was arriving home yesterday. As she was about to compliment her on her fabulous tan, Kimberley's smile vanished at the far from pleased look on Doreen Gilbert's face as she stepped over the threshold and said bluntly:

'Is it true?'

'Er—is what true?' Kimberley asked, mystified.

'I've just driven up from London. I called in at the post office for some cigarettes before I went home, and was greeted by news, talk that's all over the village, but which even now I find too unbelievable to take in.'

Knowing Doreen's caring nature, the fact that Bramcote was her second port of call even before she went to her own home after being away for nearly two months, Kimberley saw not only which piece of news she was referring to, but that she regarded it as urgent that she come and find out the truth for herself.

'You mean about Slade and me?' she said.

'Is it true?' Doreen came in hurriedly. 'That you've *married* him!'

'We were married three weeks after we met,' Kimberley said quietly, and watched as, sagging visibly, Doreen dropped to sit down.

'Oh, Kim, Kim,' she said distractedly. 'Why did you have to do that? Didn't you hear a word of anything I said to you that night before I went on holiday?'

'It's all right,' Kimberley tried to assure her, but Doreen wasn't listening.

'I *told* you—*warned* you about him! Told you he's not the marrying kind.'

'He married me.' She knew all Doreen's concern was for her, but she was beginning to feel a mite offended.

'Yes, but for how long?'

'I . . .' Kimberley couldn't find an answer.

She had thought herself many times that she couldn't wait until the day came when they would be divorced—but that was before she had spent last night alone, and had missed Slade. And now she wasn't sure about anything any more. But there was no time then to do any sorting out in her mind, for Doreen was looking at her with very sad eyes, seeming to be

fighting a battle within herself, then suddenly she was
saying:

'Kim—nobody around here knows this, but my
marriage to Edward is not my first marriage.'

'You've been married before!'

She was as much surprised by the revelation as she
was that Doreen had so suddenly forgotten the deep
concern she had felt at returning from holiday to find
her married to Slade. That was until Doreen went
on, and doubts began to creep in then that she had
forgotten nothing.

'For eight years I was married to a wife-cheating
womaniser. I suppose deep down I still feel pain from
it—that's why I never talk of it,' she said. 'I just didn't
have the least suspicion that his absences from home
were for business other than the business he told me. I
hadn't a clue until I found out differently that all the
lies I swallowed so innocently were the lies they were.
I felt ashamed when everything at last did click into
place, of the many times I'd rushed to greet him and
fuss over him. I felt defiled when I thought of the
times I'd welcomed him to my bed when he came back
from his "business trips".'

The quick sympathy that had risen in Kimberley at
the outset was numbed when Doreen had finished
speaking. 'You're hinting that Slade will start to do
the same, aren't you?' She brought out what her intelligence had seen, remembering all too easily that she
and Slade hadn't been married a week when she had
thought he had been finding solace elsewhere. He
hadn't left her overnight since, but her confidence in
her ability to hold a man was not very high, so she just
had to take note of what Doreen was saying.

'I was the last to know about my first husband,'
Doreen said unhappily. 'I just can't stand by and watch
you suffer the way I suffered.'

'You think Slade will soon get tired of me?'
Kimberley asked solemnly.

'Oh, Kim, I don't mean to be unkind, believe me I don't,' Doreen mourned. 'But if I was wrong about Slade going in for a speedy divorce, it's best you know now rather than go on for years and years living in the same cloud cuckoo land that I did.' She looked away, her caring soul unable to witness any pain her words might evoke, as she said, 'I'm afraid, love, he already has.'

'Has?' Kimberley's eyes shot wide.

And glancing at her, in a hurry now to tell her quickly and get it all said, Doreen told her, 'Edward and I flew in yesterday to the foulest weather. We were lucky, all flights after ours were diverted—to somewhere in Scotland, I think. Anyway, Edward said it was ludicrous for us to think of driving home in such conditions, so we booked into a hotel.'

'Well, we'd just finished dinner and were out of the dining room when I realised I hadn't got my lighter. Edward offered to go back for it, but I didn't see why he should—my concession to him not liking the way I puff away like a chimney. Anyway, I was just going out of the dining room again, my lighter retrieved, when tucked away in a corner I saw Slade.'

A feeling of sickness hit Kimberley even before she had the answer to her question, 'With a woman?'

Doreen nodded. 'I didn't know then that he was married to you. I remember I smiled to myself thinking "Trust Slade to be dining with the best looking woman in the room!"' So she was beautiful Kimberley, thought dully. 'I was just about to go strolling over with a "long time no see" type of remark, when suddenly the woman burst out laughing at something he said, and from the adoring way she looked up at him, from the way they were enjoying each other's company, I knew that not only was the evening not going to end there—a person would have to be thicker than thick not to see that, even without knowing Slade's reputation—I knew also that my presence would most definitely be *de trop.*'

Kimberley didn't see any reason to question any of what she had said. Now she wanted nothing more than that Doreen should go. She felt sullied already when she recalled that intimate "darling" Slade had breathed over the phone last night, and was growing furious with herself that she had for one single moment thought that tonight she would be intimating she had adjusted to having him as her husband. Fury battled with sickness as she visualised him using that same intimate 'darling' to the beautiful woman who had shared last night with him.

'Thank you for telling me,' she said, and knowing it hadn't been easy for Doreen, 'I appreciate how difficult it was for you.'

'What will you do?' Doreen asked.

'I'll think of something,' she said, forcing a smile up from the soles of her feet.

And think she did. All afternoon her mind went backwards and forwards over the same theme. Each word Doreen had uttered was repeated over and over in her mind, so that by the time it came for Slade to walk in through the door, there was nothing in her of the girl who had chatted so easily on the phone to him the night before.

Of a certainty she knew Slade Darville was going to have a very long wait if he still felt that desire for her body that had spurred him into marrying her.

That Bramcote was no longer hers disturbed her greatly, but since he had told her—and strangely, she still had trust in him about the house—that Bramcote would always be her home, then she still had her beloved Bramcote. She realised she would have to put up with him living in it too until such time as he got fed up with the situation and moved out. Perhaps they could write a fresh contract whereby she gave him his money back? That was all vague and in the future, but one thing was for sure, she would be sleeping at the Rose and Crown on Monday night—where Slade laid his head was immaterial to her.

She heard his car, thought it would be so much better if she could act, barring when he came to bed, as though Doreen's visit had never been.

But one look at his warm look as he breezed in, without the softly intimate, 'Hello, darling,' had her knowing she had to kill that look in his eye dead, before he went any farther.

'Have you eaten?' she asked him coldly.

'Shall I go out and come in again?' he asked, his voice teasing, her tone not lost on him. 'I think you must be confusing me with some other feller.'

'Go out and not come in at all would suit me very nicely,' she retorted acidly, and saw from the way his eyes narrowed that her message had reached him loud and clear.

'So what happened in between five o'clock last night and now?'

'Nothing,' she said carelessly. But she should have known by now he wouldn't let her get away with that.

'Nothing?' he repeated, his eyes steady on her. 'Nothing—in the shape of what?'

'I'll leave you to cook something,' Kimberley said. 'I've things to do upstairs.'

She nearly made it out into the hall too. Only before she could congratulate herself on escaping, Slade's hands were on her shoulders, and he was steering her into the living room.

'How many times, Kimberley,' he said, swinging her round so he could see into her face, his expression harsh, 'do I have to tell you not to go around bottling things up?' Her set look had little effect on him, as he told her brusquely, 'Get it out of your system,' and then as wilfully she stared back, his expression softened. 'Am I such a brute that you can't tell me what's happened to bring about the change?' He gave her arm a small tug. 'We've shared confidences before, haven't we? Can you no longer talk to me, Kim?'

It infuriated her that he should remind her of even the smallest confidence. Angrily she shrugged out of his hold, her anger making her tongue unwary. She had not the slightest intention of letting him know anything about Doreen Gilbert's call that day.

'There's absolutely nothing to talk about,' she snapped. 'But should I at any time have anything I want to confide in someone, then it wouldn't be to you!' And growing angrier, 'I have truer—friends—I would far rather confide in!'

A grim look came to Slade at her words. 'I thought you trusted me,' he grated, his coaxing tone gone.

She saw a look come to him then that convinced her his brain was ticking over. Though he could puzzle at it from now till Christmas and he still wouldn't come up with the right answer, she was convinced of that too. Though that conviction dipped a little when thoughtfully, slowly, he said:

'I saw Edward Gilbert today.' And, surprising her with a sharp look, 'Did you know that Doreen, the dear lady who warned you about me, if I remember correctly, has returned to Amberton?'

Kimberley's face gave her away, she knew it. She saw from Slade's expression he knew the answer before the 'Yes' she couldn't hide was forced from her. 'She came over.'

'And promptly got stuck into laying down the poison.'

'I've always found her to be truthful,' said Kimberley, ready for an argument, only to find the wind taken from her sails when Slade agreed:

'So have I.' And while she was remarshalling her forces, 'Though if you're going to hang me, I do think I have a right to know what's been said.'

He could go and take a running leap, was her first reaction, and her expression said as much. But Slade wasn't running anywhere. He was not moving. He was staying put—was waiting. Fairness prodded at her—and something akin to hope.

That was until she remembered that Doreen just wouldn't lie to her. And Slade was still waiting. He would follow her and finish this discussion upstairs if need be—she had learned that much about him.

'Do you deny,' she asked at last, 'that you dined with a beautiful woman last night?'

If she had expected him to be shamefaced in any way that he had been caught out, then Kimberley was doomed to disappointment. Straight away he was on the attack, his look harsh, as he slammed at her:

'I thought you trusted me?'

'Do you deny it,' she pressed. Even with their marriage a non-starter, since he had demanded fairness before being hanged, she was determined to hear it from his own lips.

Then she had cause to wonder what thought had occurred to him, for suddenly he was smiling. Smiling and looking so pleased with himself that she felt sick again as she no longer wondered what thought had touched him. Her challenging him, bringing to his mind his beautiful table companion, had reminded him of his enjoyment spent with that companion. And it was her turn to wait. But she didn't need the confirmation he stopped smiling long enough to own up to.

'No,' he said, with no sign of regret, 'I cannot deny my companion of last evening was a beautiful woman,' and that pleased look about him again. 'She was, in fact, a *very* beautiful woman.'

Kimberley slept badly that night. And it didn't do anything to help the irritability that awakened with her when she went downstairs and saw Slade, on the point of leaving, still looking as pleased with himself as he had when she had turned from him, and he had let her go, after he had admitted he had spent the night with a *very* beautiful woman.

'Going to send your husband off to work with a kiss?' he asked with some charm.

A sharp retort of 'Go to hell' came near the surface, but she bit it back. 'Only if you're promising not to come back,' she said, sugar dripping—and felt better when she saw that had taken some of the arrogance out of him. Though his voice had a fair amount of honey in it too as he bade her goodbye with:

'Don't push it, sweetheart—you might get lucky!'

Bigheaded swine! she thought the moment the door had closed, and wondered what it was about him that, even in her irritation, his smart reply had her lips wanting to twitch.

Doreen rang during the morning inviting her for coffee. And had Kimberley thought their conversation over coffee could be kept strictly to talk about her friend's holiday, then she would have loved to have accepted. But although she liked Doreen more than ever because over the phone she didn't refer to her visit yesterday, but settled for a troubled, 'Are you all right, Kim?' she thought it best to refuse.

'I'm fine,' she said sunnily. 'Will you let me off coffee today?' And hurrying on before Doreen could get a word in, she explained about the builders coming in on Monday, and the work they had to do, telling her about curtains that had to be taken down, about furniture that wasn't going to be moved out that had to be covered in dust-sheets.

'You're staying at Bramcote while all this work is being done?' Doreen asked, her mind safely taken away from her concern for her, Kimberley thought.

But she saw then that to tell her she intended seeking a bed at the Rose and Crown would have Doreen offering to have her stay with her for however long it took until she could move back into her home. She hated lying to her, but didn't have time to think up anything tactful that would ensure her feelings weren't hurt.

'We're moving to Slade's place in London,' she said, presenting herself with a problem of some time contacting Doreen and telling her she had decided against London.

'I see,' said Doreen slowly. And from that thoughtful 'I see' Kimberley saw she had taken it that she was going to disregard what she had told her yesterday.

Kimberley came away from the phone wondering why she hadn't told Doreen that Slade had brazenly owned up that he had spent the night with his beautiful companion.

It couldn't be that she felt some sort of loyalty to him, could it? she wondered, her brow wrinkling. Her brow cleared as she scoffed at the idea. Yet as the day wore on into the afternoon she was frowning again as the realisation came that to further blacken Slade's name by telling Doreen anything of what had passed between them last night was something she just could not do.

Now why should it bother her what anyone thought of him? An hour later she discovered just exactly why—and never had she thought to receive such a shock.

She had been clearing out upstairs, when around three, and for the umpteenth time, she made yet another trip outside to the dustbin. Why she looked up at the gate just then she didn't know—probably attracted by the sound of someone talking, she later thought. But she did look, and as her stomach knotted up, she kept on looking, couldn't take her eyes from the gate. For the man who a year ago had written and told her he had fallen in love with someone else, had asked her to release him from their engagement, was coming through it!

Colour surged to her face as vaguely she registered old Sammy, a bundle of assorted pieces of wood under his arm denoting that he had been wood-gathering, passing by the hedge an unusual gleeful look on his face. That gleeful look told her since David never spoke to him, that he must have made some comment to David that delighted him to have made.

Her cheeks were pale by the time David reached her. He was in civilian clothes, but his military bearing that she had so loved was obvious.

'David,' she said, collecting herself and holding out her hand.

He smiled, that familiar smile she knew and had loved. She waited for her heart to flip the way it always did when he smiled—but nothing happened.

'Hello, precious,' he said, but that 'precious', that at one time would have thrilled her, now left her cold. 'How are you?' he asked, a familiar seductive note there as he leant forward and aimed a kiss at her mouth. His kiss landed on her cheek, because just at that moment Kimberley moved.

The imprint of his lips still warm on her cheek, she was dazed to find it had aroused not one iota of emotion in her. She wasn't even angry that after so long an absence he could calmly come to her home and act so familiarly. I'm indifferent to him! she thought, and was shattered at the truth of that thought. She stared at him, at the smiling handsome features of the man it seemed impossible now she had nearly had a nervous breakdown over.

'I'm fine—fine,' she said, gathering her wits together.

'I should have telephoned you before coming,' said David, smiling again as though never for a moment doubting she would welcome him any time he chose to call. 'I can see my arriving out of the blue has shaken you.' He smiled again and looked towards the door, clearly expecting to be invited in.

'Why did you come?' she asked, not moving.

'A couple of reasons,' he said. 'I haven't been home

for some time, as you probably know.' His conceit surprised her. She had never thought him conceited before. But clearly he was of the opinion she had spies out the whole of the time logging his movements and reporting back to her. 'This is the first chance I've had to come over and tell you how very, very sorry I was to hear about your father.'

If he was so very sorry, a letter saying as much wouldn't have hurt him, Kimberley found herself thinking. But so indifferent did she feel towards him, it seemed too much trouble to mention it.

Since he didn't seem in any hurry to go, and not wanting him inside her home, unconcerned whether he thought her ill-mannered or not, she sought round for something to say—a clear indication that one or other of them had changed a great deal this last year, or that they had never had very much in common anyway. She had never had to try to make conversation with him before!

'Let's go into the orchard,' he suggested, when he saw no invitation inside the house was forthcoming.

'Why not?' she shrugged, moving away from him.

She felt absolutely nothing for him. She realised she would much sooner have his room than his company, and wished—wished Slade was here. Her thoughts faltered. Slade, Slade would—Slade would tell him where to get off. A riot started inside her as she realised just how protected she felt with Slade. But it—it wasn't just that. She swallowed, saw David had halted at the exact spot he had once proposed, and she had not even noticed it.

She saw he had observed the way she had swallowed and knew he had misread the reason for it, but was so shocked by the revelation that had just come to her that his over-confident smile barely registered.

More than ever she didn't want him here. She wanted, needed, to be by herself. She had to be by herself to try to deny what she knew to be so unmistakably true!

'We—is your wife with you on this trip?' she asked, finding the question out of thin air, not interested in his answer, but needing to say something that might take that mawkish look off his face.

'I'm not married.'

'Oh?' said Kimberley politely, vague memories stirring in the background of the nights she had cried herself to sleep thinking of him married to someone else.

'I made a mistake,' he confessed. And beaming smugly, 'I discovered I didn't really love her after all.'

'A good job you found out before you married, then, isn't it?' she said, her thoughts wanting to fly back to Slade, and David taking hold of her right hand irritating her.

'I discovered I never ever fell out of love with you,' he said, which had her leaving her thoughts to stare at him in amazement.

She had pictured this scene so many times in those early days, those sleepless nights. She had wanted it so badly to happen, that he should fall out of love with the woman he had thrown her over for, that he should come back to her. But now it was actually happening, the moment here when many times she had visualised herself melting into his arms, all Kimberley could do was to stare at him and wonder what it was she had ever seen in him in the first place.

'I told you I had another reason for coming to see you,' he went on. And while she was staring he let go of her right hand, ferreted around in his trouser pocket and brought out the engagement ring she had returned to him twelve months ago. 'This ring should never have left your finger,' he said.

And confidently, while she was too dumb struck by what was happening to make any protest, he took hold of her left hand, raised it and went to put the ring back on her finger.

The sight of her wedding ring knocked him for six,

she could see that. 'You're married!' he exclaimed, his
jaw dropping comically as he lifted his dumbfounded
eyes to her face. He was near to gibbering then as he
rattled out, 'That old tramp, Sammy Smith, told me
you were, but I thought he was just having a go at me
when he said your husband would give me a fourpenny
one if he saw me near you.'

Kimberley had to smile. She could just see old
Sammy saying it. But her smile had to be restrained
when she found, even with the evidence of her wedding
ring there, that David was still not believing the nine-
teen-year-old girl who had been so besotted over him
could have married someone else.

'Tell me it's not true, my precious. Tell me you love
me and no one else.'

'It is true. I am married,' said Kimberley solemnly,
working hard to keep her face straight, her innate sensitivity having her knowing David's vanity would be
sorely bruised if she laughed at him and his astonishment that she should dare to stop loving for him.
Soberness came to her as she told him, 'And no, David,
I don't love you.' For how could she love him, when
her heart and every living part of her was in love with
the man she had married? She loved Slade, and her
love for David had never been a love like this.

'But you've got to love me,' he was protesting. 'You
didn't refer to it in the letter you sent returning my
ring, but I knew you always would.'

David had taken some convincing, Kimberley
thought after he had gone. He had strutted away eventually like some wounded peacock. But not before he
had had the audacity to suggest, since he knew she
couldn't possibly be in love with her husband, that she
leave him and go with him. She had grown angry then,
had been, she thought, a shade pompous herself as she
had told him in no uncertain terms that the promises
she made were obviously of sterner stuff than his.

But were they? she thought dejectedly. She had

promised herself to Slade, yet their marriage was still not the normal marriage he wanted. And with the fact that he had spent the night before last with some other female hitting her hard, how could she ever keep her promise now?

While David had been with her there had been no time to think. But she had too much time before Slade was due home in which to do some thinking. And how was she ever to keep from him that somehow, God knew how, for she couldn't fathom it, she had fallen heart and soul in love with him?

It had taken seeing David again to show her where her true feelings lay. Though when she considered that sickness that had invaded her when Slade had openly told her about his beautiful woman friend, she realised she would soon have got there without any help seeing David again had given her. She had been jealous, she still was—and it hurt.

Kimberley had many hours of painful, gut-tearing jealousy to go through before Slade came home. The fact that he was later home that night than usual had her certain he had made a detour to be with his very beautiful companion of two evenings ago.

Never had she known such terrible emotional trauma. Her love for him, her imagination at him sharing with some other woman so much as a smile had her fighting to keep tears at bay.

At nine o'clock, her ears strained from listening for the sound of his car, she heard him pull up outside, and was then in so much of a dither, she didn't know how she was going to face him.

If she had been hoping, in those agonising hours of waiting, that once she saw him again she would find she didn't love him after all, then the moment she laid eyes on him Kimberley knew she had been hoping in vain. For even though his face was stern, as if something had gone wrong with his day, she knew he was the one and only man for her—and she had no idea how she was going to contend with it.

She wanted to make some snappy remark like, 'Fancy—you remembered where you live!' But she couldn't speak. She was afraid something in her voice would betray that she wanted to fling her arms around him, beg him to forget all other women, to let him know she would be his whenever he desired her. Afraid her eyes would give her away, Kimberley couldn't hold that flint-hard look he bestowed on her.

'Is there any reason you can't look me in the eye?' were his first words. Not very pleasant-sounding words either, as with his usual 'shame the devil' tactics Slade had seen anyway that something was wrong and wasn't hesitating to bring it out into the open.

'N-no reason at all,' she said huskily, knowing that this was one time he would have to put her on the rack before she would come out into the open, tell him she loved him—and not then.

She kept her eyes lowered when she heard the grating of a kitchen chair she had left in the way. She knew Slade had unceremoniously moved it aside, and braced herself as he came over to her. Her nerves stretched to screaming as unspeaking he stood in front of her. Then quietly, breathing deeply, he said:

'I gave old Sammy a lift up from the crossroads. He tells me you had a visitor this afternoon.'

Her head shot up at that, hope ridiculous in her heart that Slade was being tough with her because he was jealous. Then the hope went plummeting back to where it came from. He wasn't jealous, she could see that. There was nothing but distaste emitting from those eyes, a definite navy blue now, that on coming home he had been informed by the village poacher that his wife had been entertaining her ex-fiancé in his absence.

But she had done nothing wrong, and she made her eyes stay on his. But in doing so, in meeting his piercing scrutiny, she couldn't help that the secret locked up in her had her blushing.

'So Bennet *has* been smelling around your skirts,'
Slade snapped, and had she not felt anger flame into
life at his choice of expression, Kimberley would have
known fear from the aggression that was building up
in him.

'David called, yes,' she said shortly, and saw an explosion was imminent as Slade's jaw jutted and his
nostrils flared at her words. But she could have no
idea the explosion was going to come from her, as
fiercely, he grated:

'And is that blush indicative that you were able to
adjust more quickly to him than you've been able to
adjust to me?'

For two seconds Kimberley didn't get his meaning.
And then the shock of what he was asking—had she,
that afternoon, been to bed with David?—had her
reacting violently.

'Don't judge me by your own vile standards!' came
spilling from her, at the same time her hand came
flashing, as she struck him a terrible blow across the
face.

Her hand stinging from the blow she had struck him,
Kimberley felt the hard grip of his hands on her arms.
Her face ashen she saw from the fury in him she had
just pushed Slade Darville too far.

Her own fury vanished, and fear replaced it, as she
knew that Slade's mouth would soon be savage on hers,
no tenderness there, that he wouldn't stop there.
Shaking that she had brought this on herself by serving
him that terrible blow, she felt his brutal grip on her
arms intensify, and thought her bones would break as
Slade fought a losing battle for control.

She saw his teeth clench tightly, then hardly daring
to believe it she saw he had mastered his temper. She
felt relief surge in that he wasn't going to take her in
anger when his arms dropped to his sides. But she was
left with a feeling that any movement she made to run

from him would have him hauling her back, that hard-fought-for control lost. Wanting desperately to flee. Kimberley stood rooted. Then she heard his voice, rasping with the control he was exercising.

'Go,' he said, an anger showing in his eyes that terrified her. 'Get out of my sight,' he gritted. 'If I see you again before morning, I promise you the retribution you're expecting will be mine.'

Kimberley didn't wait for any more. She fled. She was shaking so violently, she had difficulty in opening her bedroom door.

It proved a long night for her. Where Slade slept she didn't know, for he didn't enter her room to cross to the dressing room. At dawn she switched off the bedside lamp, a sadness in her that went too deep for tears. She had learned a good deal about herself this past year. She had recently learned many things about Slade too. She had learned to love him, and not just because he had taught her to laugh again. He had bossed her about, seen to it that she ate, made her furious at times. But oh, how she loved him!

And yet, for her own peace of mind, there was only one way left open to her. Even if she could bear to share him with his other women, she knew her frailties too well. She knew she couldn't stay with him waiting, expecting every day, for him to tell her, 'Nice knowing you', or whatever phrase he used to the women he tired of. She loved him—loved him so much, it went deeper than her love for Bramcote.

CHAPTER TEN

AFRAID that if she saw Slade again her resolve to leave him might be weakened, Kimberley stayed in her room until she heard his car pull away, indicating that he had left for his office.

The very fact he had gone off to work without so much as seeking her out, endorsed for her she was right to go. She needed no other sign that already he was growing tired of her. It was with a heavy heart that she pulled out the largest of her suitcases. She had no intention of coming back for anything. An hour later she left Bramcote.

Why she chose to go to London she didn't know. But sitting in her hotel room later that day, she realised it was because London was where Slade worked. She could be near him in the city; and yet be lost in it. Anonymous.

Not that Slade would come looking for her, she thought, glancing at her watch. Left him she might have, but her thoughts all centred on him. If he wasn't staying late in London with one of his 'friends', then in ten minutes he would be arriving at Bramcote, to find her gone.

She recalled that day, that first day after their marriage when she had disappeared for the whole day. She recalled how furious Slade had been with her when she had eventually turned up, and remembered that she had promised to tell him where she was going if ever again she felt the need to disappear.

For the next ten minutes her sensitivities were pulled this way and that. She hadn't so much as left him a note! Would he be concerned? Go out looking for her as he had before?

No, of course he wouldn't, she told herself. But as ten minutes turned into eleven, and then twelve, Kimberley was a mass of indecision as to what to do.

She knew she would go weak at the knees at just the sound of his voice. Yet supposing—just supposing he was worried by her not being there—though annoyed more than worried was probably what he would be at her thoughtlessness in just disappearing, she thought. He had told her he thought her his responsibility, but . . .

Fed up with the way her agitated thoughts were see-sawing, she picked up the phone to get it over with. Then she found it was customary in the hotel she was staying in for the telephonist to get the number for her and to ring her back.

Kimberley gave the Amberton number and replaced the receiver, half of her wishing she had left things as they were.

The telephonist was taking an age. So Slade wasn't in, she thought, sickness gnawing away at her that for the second night in succession he was in no hurry to go home.

The phone jangled, and her nerves were so all over the place, she nearly leapt out of her skin. Her voice was thin and reedy when she managed an eventual, 'Hello?'

'Your call, madam,' said the telephonist, and clicked off the line.

'H-hello,' Kimberley stammered.

'Kim! Kimberley—where are you?'

'I'm——' she hesitated, then realised he would never find her in London even if it entered his head to start looking. 'I'm in London,' she said.

'What the *hell* are you doing there?' he asked, a fine aggression coming through.

'I—I've left you,' she said, and had to gulp before she said the next bit, which even to her own ears sounded inane in the extreme. 'I forgot to leave you a note.'

She expected to hear him coming roaring back at her with some cutting remark on the lines that he wasn't the bloody milkman—it would have been in keeping. But he didn't. He didn't say anything in the lengthy silence that followed, which had her thinking he was so uninterested he had gone.

Then she heard his voice coming through again, not roaring, not sarcastic, but unbelievably mild, aggression gone, as quietly he asked:

'You didn't think maybe we should talk it over?'

Panic hit her that he was sounding logical. She knew him and his talking things out. He always had had a knack of getting right to the bottom of things. She couldn't bear that he should know how idiotically she had fallen in love with him.

'No,' she said. And before he could reply, she had put down the phone.

She had eaten nothing that day. She had been toying with the idea of going down to dinner, but just hearing Slade's voice, wanting to be back with him, had any trace of appetite vanishing. She would have to begin making plans soon, she thought, going back to sink down into one of the two easy chairs in the room, but not yet, not just yet.

The receptionist had asked her when she had booked in how long she was staying, but she hadn't been sure about that either. 'May I let you know? My plans are flexible,' she had said. Flexible! They were non-existent. Where did she go from here?

Kimberley was still sitting in the chair she had sunk into, when about an hour after her phone call to Slade there was a knock at the door. Listlessly she got up to answer it, good manners making her have a polite smile ready if this was the sort of hotel where they came to turn the bed down each night.

She opened the door, and her smile froze. Slade, still in his business suit, stood there. His face equally unsmiling, he studied her as she took a step back, then came into the room.

'What—are you doing here?' she gasped. And trying desperately to collect herself, 'H-how did you know where—where to find me?'

'The hotel telephonist gave me the name of the hotel before she connected us, you supplied the rest.'

Kimberley groaned inwardly. Slade always would be so much smarter than she. 'Why have you come?' she asked, knowing she was going to have to cut him off short if he was determined to have everything out in the open.

He looked at her, the ice in his eyes chilling her as bluntly he stated, 'I thought I should tell you personally that I don't intend to divorce you in order for you to marry Bennet.'

How she kept from showing the shock with which his remark hit her, she never knew. For she was staggered that Slade should think she had left him for—David! She lowered her eyes, her face this time giving nothing away.

'Who asked you to?' she found enough stiffening to ask, and flicking a glance to him saw her question had shaken him. But it was only for a brief while. Then his aggression was to the fore, and he was asking in return, his eyes glinting:

'You'll live with him while married to me?'

A spurt of anger wouldn't be denied that *he* was daring to moralise to *her*. 'I'll do as I please,' she retorted resentfully.

'You'll lose Bramcote.'

'I—I just don't care any more,' she said—and saw then that she could talk so of her beloved home had come near to rocking him where he stood. It had killed his aggression at any rate, for his voice was quiet, when he said:

'He means *that* much to you?'

'I . . .' she began. Then, as once before, she found it

impossible to lie to him.

She turned her back on him, wishing he would go, kept her back ramrod-stiff as she waited for him to start trying to prise everything into the open. Then she heard him move, and braced herself.

But she need not have bothered, for she didn't feel a hand come to grip her shoulder. She did not feel herself turned, made to face him, but instead heard the door behind her quietly close.

She did turn then, voluntarily—to find he had gone. And she wished with all her heart he was back there with her.

The reality that he had gone, that never would she see him again, was debilitating. He had driven all the way back to London solely, she knew now, to tell her he wasn't divorcing her—though had he not done so he would have realised soon enough that she wouldn't be making the first moves to be free. Her pride surfaced. Perhaps it was a good thing he had called. Wasn't it just as well he had gone off thinking that David Bennet still held her heart?

Eventually Kimberley went to bed. Never in her life had she ever felt so alone, so alone and bereft. She had thought she had known the pain of losing someone before. But oh, dear God, it had never been like this.

Exhausted from lack of sleep the night before, she at last found rest from the unhappiness that was eating into her, in several hours' sleep.

She was glad she had ordered early morning tea, and drank thirstily before getting out of bed and willing herself to face another day. A day bleak, as all days were to be from now on without seeing or hearing Slade.

That first day stretched endlessly in front of her, hours yet to be got through until she could return to her bed and hope for a few more hours of oblivion. She went down to breakfast simply because she saw it as one way of killing some of the ample time at her disposal.

The chambermaid had already attended to her room when after breakfast Kimberley took the lift back up to her floor. So she couldn't think why anyone should come knocking at her door shortly after she had returned to it. Knowing with heart-tearing certainty that she had seen the last of Slade, she went to answer the knock, never giving thought that it might be him.

Open-mouthed, she stared at the figure in navy sweater and dark slacks who stood there. Her heart beat wildly against her ribs. Slade should be business-suited and at his office, went through her head as, nearly dropping to see him there, she strove to wake up her brain and wonder why he had thought it necessary to pay her a second visit.

'Wh ... ' was as far as she got. Her voice died as she saw the determination about him. It worried her. She had seen that look before.

Slade wasn't waiting for her to find her voice again, but did no more than stretch out his hands to move her to one side. Then calmly he was stepping into her room, and was closing the door after him with a deliberation that seemed to match. He then turned, and for an age just stood looking at her with those dark blue eyes she knew so well.

'Why have—you come?' she managed to get out.

'You're looking a shade more rested than you did last night, though you're still too pale,' he observed, which was no answer at all, and had her repeating:

'Why have you come, Slade?'

'I would have returned last night after I'd been to see Bennet,' he said, stupefying her anew, 'but you looked so done in when I called, I thought it best you had your rest rather than get you out of bed at midnight.'

So her previous night without sleep had showed. But that hardly impinged on her consciousness. 'You've been to see David?' she asked, stunned.

'Did you think I wouldn't?' he asked, aggression only just beneath the surface. 'Did you honestly think I would let some other man come in and take my wife without doing something about it?'

How possessive that sounded! Had she not known differently she would have thought Slade meant he would never let her go. But she did know differently. Without having the least idea why he should suddenly show he had a possessive streak in him, she knew it wouldn't last.

And then any delving her mind would have done into why he should feel even briefly possessive about her went skidding as she recalled the way she had virtually sent David away with a flea in his ear. Slade must know that too, since he had been to see him!

And it was agitation only that was inside her then, because that left her without any good reason for leaving Slade—and that she realised was exactly why he was here—to find out why!

'I—er—didn't think you would—er—go and see David,' she said stiltedly at last.

'That much became obvious within a very few minutes of my talking to him,' he said, leaving her to guess his aggression must have been out in full force, when he looked levelly at her, and went on, 'It didn't take him very long to tell me he never intended seeing you again because you'd told him you no longer loved him. That you, Kimberley Darville, no longer wanted him.'

He had left her without a leg to stand on. Helplessly she looked at him. Last night she had thought, having led him to think she had left him because of her love for David, that she had come out of this with her pride intact. But Slade knew now that that wasn't true.

'Are you going to tell me what all this is about?' he asked, his eyes not missing she was floundering.

'I—er . . .' she began, searching round for any lie that might deviate him from that look in his eye, for all his aggression had gone, that said he was insisting on the truth.

'Is it that you hate me so much you would prefer to lose the house you love rather than stay with me?'

Kimberley dropped her eyes and stared miserably at the carpet. Slade was waiting for an answer, and she—couldn't lie. 'I don't—hate you,' she said, her voice barely above a whisper.

'What, then?'

She couldn't answer that one. She didn't want him to go, but she couldn't bear that he should stay and badger at her like this. Yet he was waiting. Waiting with that patience in him that would endure if he had to wait all day.

But he wasn't waiting all day. With astonishment she heard, from a toughness that had entered his voice, that his patience with her had worn thin, was wearing thinner the longer it took her to reply.

'Don't you think you owe it to me to give me an answer?' he challenged. Then, his voice quieting again, 'Be honest with me. Even if it hurts, be honest. It's—important to me.'

Dumbly she raised her eyes, and saw Slade was watching her intently. He looked strained, as though he too had missed some sleep. Her voice was husky, her words jerky.

'I—had to—leave you,' she said.

'Why, Kim?' he asked, his eyes never leaving her face.

She swallowed, cleared her throat. She saw then how she had short changed him. She had married him to gain Bramcote. But what had he gained? Nothing. She had withheld her body from him when that had been his reason for marrying her. And while it was true she had sold Bramcote to him, he need not have bought it. He could, she thought, have just as easily allowed it to crumble. Yet he hadn't. He had bought a house he probably didn't want, and had given her his word that it would always be her home. And she knew she could rely on his word too, for even though mightily provoked when she had hit him, he had controlled his temper, kept his word that he would wait until she could come to him willingly.

Oh yes, she had more than short-changed him. He had said she owed him an explanation, but she owed him more than that. He had asked her to be honest with him—even if it hurt. And it was going to hurt, she knew that. This was one time when to stay and discuss rather than bottle things up was going to be more painful to her than any of the discussions they had so far had. Yet she owed him—and it was going to crucify her to be as honest as he wanted.

'I . . .' she began, then found she couldn't tell him anything while he was looking at her. She turned from him. 'I loved David,' she said, her breathing not any easier that she couldn't see Slade's face. 'When—when he threw me over I nearly had a nervous breakdown.' She cleared her throat again. 'It was because of my love for him that—that first night of our marriage that I—I couldn't . . .' Her voice gave out.

'That you couldn't give yourself to me,' Slade finished for her, his voice close, telling her that although she had taken a couple of steps from him, he had moved too, and was right behind her.

Kimberley nodded. 'Yes,' she said huskily, then felt hands on her shoulders, felt herself being turned until she was facing him.

'Go on,' he insisted quietly.

Her throat dry, she swallowed again. 'I don't know what it is about me, but—but where my emotions are concerned, I—I don't appear to do things halfheartedly. Th-the way I was attached to Bramcote . . .'

'But Bramcote is no longer your first love,' he reminded her. And she couldn't deny it, for hadn't she told him last night that she no longer cared about the house any more? 'Neither, so you've told Bennet,'

Slade said slowly when she remained silent, 'is he.'

Her palms grew moist. Slade would get there on his own, she wouldn't have to tell him. But he couldn't have, she realised a moment later, because demanding he certainly was, but unnecessarily cruel never. And yet he went on to prompt:

'So . . .'

Kimberley gave a small cough, her throat constricted again. Then with her eyes fixed on his sweater, she began, 'I've—I've told you it nearly broke me when David threw me over.' She took a deep breath, striving for calm that just wasn't there, and had to say it then because she couldn't take much more of this soul-baring. 'I left Bramcote because—because I didn't think I could take it when you too threw me over.'

The whole room seemed hushed after her words had fallen. Slade never so much as moved a muscle, and she knew then that he hadn't worked it out for himself, that her words had stunned him. So quiet was it in the room, she even heard him swallow, before, his voice thick in his throat, he asked the question:

'Are you saying you—have some—feeling—for me?'

More brave than she had ever been, Kimberley raised her eyes to his taut waiting expression. She knew then it had to be a full confession, a confession that, when he heard it, would have him going out of her life for ever.

Tears had already started to her eyes, when grabbing all her courage, she looked at him squarely and said quietly, simply:

'I love you, Slade.'

The way his jaw clenched, the colour that came up under his skin, the look that came to him, told her her love for him was an embarrassment he had never thought of. And tears were streaming down her face when she could do no other than put her back to him. She had to have it all said then. Should he still desire her, overcome his embarrassment and still want her, then he had to know just how it was with her.

She gulped for air in the awful shocked silence behind her. 'I love you so much nothing else matters, not even Bramcote,' she told him chokily. 'But I just can't live with you—h-have you love my body for a short while until you get tired of me.' She broke off to swallow tears. 'That would finish me, Slade. I just know it would.' She wiped at her wet eyes with her hand, and tried hard for a laugh that didn't quite come off. 'You asked me for honesty, Slade—I don't think I can be more honest than that.'

The hands that came to her shoulders then were hard, but they made no move to turn her round, as gripping convulsively, his voice low, Slade said into her ears:

'Your experience with Bennet has taken away the confidence the beautiful woman you are should have. Without looking farther than your doctor friend you should know that not every man is blind to the prize Bennet didn't appreciate until too late.'

Tears rained down her face as what Slade was saying sorted itself out in her head. By saying not every man was blind, he was telling her he still wanted her.

'Don't, Slade, please don't,' she begged. 'I—I've told you about my feelings for you. But it—it just wouldn't be fair of you to make me complete my end of the bargain, when you know how I feel about you.'

'What bargain is this, my darling?' he asked, his 'my darling' bruising her because it meant nothing to him.

'You know,' she choked. 'Don't make me—go to bed with you. I've told you what it will do to me when you grow tired of me.'

'You think I would ever grow tired of you? Don't you . . .'

'Please!' Unable to bear it, Kimberley cut him off. 'Already you've grown tired of waiting,' she reminded him—and couldn't understand, when he was the one who had always insisted on straight talking, that he should then proceed to pretend otherwise.

'When did I do that?' he asked. 'I'll admit there've been times when I've despaired . . .'

A stiffness came to her that he should be this way, and again she cut him off. 'I've been totally honest with you,' she said rigidly, 'and it's been painful. Please do me the courtesy of being honest back.' And, not allowing him to interrupt, 'You know *I know* that the night you couldn't get home because of the fog, you spent it with another woman who . . .'

'Who happens to be my secretary,' Slade managed to get in, attempting to turn her to face him.

But jealousy was making a successful attack on Kimberley's other emotions as she thought of the very beautiful woman he had been with, and she refused to be turned.

'And who just happens to be beautiful,' she said, not for a moment believing it was his secretary.

'There's no law that says a woman can't be good-looking and efficient at the same time, sweetheart,' said Slade. Then gently, 'As for honesty—I admit I could have told you about Norma Milton before—but,' he broke off for a brief second, then told her, 'well, if I'm to be as totally honest as you have been, my dear——' He broke off again, only this time, before he went on, Kimberley felt the lightest of kisses float down to her nape. It had her confused, dimmed the jealousy that had been in her. 'I'll admit,' he continued, 'that when I did come home, saw what I thought might be a shade of green in your eyes . . .'

'Green!' Kimberley whispered, seeing again how much smarter than her Slade was, for she had not recognised the feelings inside her then as jealousy.

'You'll forgive me if I couldn't help hoping that you might be a tiny bit jealous. I discounted after my visit here last night that jealousy had touched you at all,' Slade went on. 'But at the time I thought, My God, Kim's jealous, she doesn't know it, but she's jealous.

And it was the best news I'd had in a long time. I
thought . . .' But Kimberley had gone rigid in his grip.
It communicated itself to him, and he left what he had
been going to say, and said instead, 'To get back to
that foggy night. The lady I dined with was my secretary—a married lady who happens to be devoted to
her husband and family, and who was feeling a touch
aggrieved when because we were working late and the
fog thickened, she couldn't get home.'

He made another attempt to get her to turn round,
and this time Kimberley did move. She wanted to see
into his face. She knew she was gullible where he was
concerned, but she thought she might see the truth if
she looked into his eyes.

'Oh, my little love,' he said softly when he saw her
tear-drenched face, and taking out his handkerchief,
he tenderly wiped her tears away.

'You were telling me about your secretary,' she
reminded him, taking a step back. That soothing note
in his voice was weakening her.

Slade looked loath to return to what he had been
saying, though since there wasn't anything else he
could want to discuss either, Kimberley felt the stir-
rings of surprise that he was staying at all, and not
only that, but that he seemed prepared to tell her all
that she wanted to know. He smiled, doing nothing for
the hold she was trying to get on herself, then
resumed:

'Norma Milton is a gem of a secretary, but, efficient
though she is in the office, she's a bit of a pain out of
it.'

'That wasn't what I heard,' she muttered, and felt
the warmth of his smile again as he went on to tell her:

'It was probably because I have my sensitivities too,
although at this moment I can see you won't believe it.
That with Norma Milton sitting glumly across from
me at dinner, her mind more with her husband and
two youngsters than on me I assure you, I did every-

thing bar stand on my head to get a smile out of her. We'd just about finished eating when finally I succeeded.'

'That must have been when Doreen saw you,' came from Kimberley. Then, remembering, 'She said your companion was looking up at you adoringly.'

'More likely trying to get me in focus. She doesn't wear her glasses out of the office, although she's as blind as a bat without them,' he said, then went on, 'Our mutual friend Doreen should have stayed around. It couldn't have been very long after that that I escorted Norma to collect her key, then saw her to the lift.'

'You didn't go in the lift with her, share her room?' The question wouldn't stay down, even though, having left him, she knew she had no right to question him. Then she found he wasn't objecting, that his patience had returned and it was remarkable, especially since he was his own man, that he wasn't hesitating to give her every last explanation to all she asked.

'Because I'd asked her to work late, and with hotels filling up fast with so many people staying in town, I saw it as my duty to see she had a comfortable room for the night, that she wasn't missing her dinner on account of it. For that reason I went to the hotel with her, dined with her, but after that I reckoned I'd done my stint. She went up to her room—I went to my London home, and there I stayed.' The corners of his mouth tilted, as he added softly, 'I stayed alone, Kim, and spent the rest of the evening wondering if you would think I was some kind of nut if I rang you for no other reason than I wanted to hear your voice.'

'You—wanted to hear my voice!' she exclaimed, staggered, then tried to oust the joy she felt that he should have said so. The situation hadn't changed. She had been right for her own peace of mind to leave him—though she saw now that she could have saved herself a lot of anguish if she had taken a leaf from his

book and asked him more about his dinner companion
that night instead of bottling it all up.

She hadn't been aware that Slade had closed in, but
suddenly he was close to her, had trailed a gentle finger
down the side of her face. 'I was lonesome for you that
night, my darling,' he said softly. 'I wanted to be there
in that leaky old house with you.'

Gently he gathered her into his arms. And there was
no thought in her as she rested her head against his
chest of resisting. She needed him to hold her, if only
for a moment. She found a small peace in the haven of
his arms, but knew it couldn't go on.

Slowly she eased away, but found, though his hold
had loosened, he was refusing to release her entirely.
'Thank you for telling me all this,' she said. 'I know
you didn't want to.' She gave him a sad smile. 'But in
view—of what I told you . . .'

'About you being in love with me?' he asked, his
eyes warm on her.

Dumbly Kimberley nodded. She didn't want him
looking at her like that, not now when she had a very
important question to ask. 'Yes,' she said. 'In view of
that, will you let me off?'

'Let you off?' he asked, his head going to one side
endorsing that he hadn't grasped her meaning.

'Will you divorce me without making me fulfil the—
terms of our bargain?'

His look of puzzlement vanished, and she could no
longer look at him. For if he should say no, she didn't
know how she was going to cope afterwards. Her head
went down again to his chest.

'You're asking me to divorce you without making
you mine, is that right?' she heard him ask.

'Please,' she said, tears starting to her eyes again as
she kept her head buried. 'Will you go now, and . . .
and forget me?'

She felt the arms holding her tighten. 'Oh, Kim, my
Kim,' he said, his voice thick with emotion. 'I know

the faith you had in yourself has been pulverised, but please, my little love, please have a little faith in me.'

Not knowing what he was meaning, nowhere near to understanding that exquisitely tender note there, Kimberley felt his hand turning her face up as he made her look at him.

And then she was barely able to breathe, because if she wasn't mistaken, and she must be, Slade was looking at her as if he absolutely adored her. 'What . . .' escaped her, while the knowledge sped in that she had to be wrong, utterly wrong.

'You're truthful friend wasn't lying when she told you about the—freedom I enjoyed as a bachelor,' he said, his adoring look staying on her. 'But believe me, my beautiful Kim, when I tell you I gave up that freedom willingly, that I haven't so much as given any woman a second look from the moment I saw you.'

And while she looked at him, unable to utter one syllable, her heart beating a crazy rhythm, his hand cupped her face, and he told her:

'My own true love, I took one look at you at the Gilberts' party and for me that was it. I fell in love with you.'

'You fell . . .?' Kimberley was reeling. But even though she wanted with everything in her to believe what he was saying, the letdown would be too great if he explained what the joke was. 'That's not funny,' she said, tight-lipped. 'As I recall it you were enjoying yourself too much dancing with the most attractive women there to even remember you'd previously introduced yourself to me.'

'Dearest Kim,' Slade said softly, his manner not changing at her challenging his statement. 'I hope soon to convince you how much you mean to me. I hope before too long that the confidence in you that has taken such a beating will find a firm foothold in knowing my love for you.' He smiled, a smile that had her legs wobbly, doubt that she might be wrong wanting to be sent on its way. 'I may have danced with a few ladies, I can't clearly remember. What I can recall is that after the way you'd looked at me with your nose in the air, I was trying to appear as normal as I could, while at the same time racking my brains for the best way to get through your frosty exterior.'

Her eyes brimming, Kimberley so wanted to believe him. She recalled too the way she had been at that first meeting. She *had* been frosty, she remembered, he hadn't lied to her about that. She had snubbed him. Yet—yet Slade, a man no one would snub twice, had come back for more.

'Oh, Slade,' she said tremulously, the hope in her heart overflowing, 'I do want to believe you.'

Gently he bent and kissed away a tear that trembled on her eyelashes. 'Believe me, my sweet darling,' he breathed. She was half way there, but another doubt presented itself. 'What is it?' he asked, his look encouraging. 'Don't bottle it up, Kim. There'll be no secrets between us from now on.'

She swallowed at the depth of tenderness he was showing her, then realised he was right. If she was ever to gain that confidence he spoke of, then anything that was worrying her had to be brought out into the open, had to be aired so her trust in his love for her could find that foothold.

'We hadn't been married above t-two days when—when you were spending the day in London,' she said huskily.

'I wasn't seeking what you were denying me elsewhere,' he said, seeing straight away what was in her mind.

And it was blissful to her not only to hear that, but to feel the caress of his lips whisper down on hers. But he drew back, his expression controlled.

'I want to kiss you so badly, my dear,' he told her. 'But first I think it's essential to you that I clear any skeletons you think may be lingering in my cupboard.'

A tender hand came to brush her forehead, and then he was telling her with a sincerity she couldn't doubt, 'I knew I was in love with you on the day we were married. What I didn't know, never having experienced such emotion before, was the depth of my love for you. I discovered that the very next day.'

'When I went missing?' she asked quietly.

'When you went missing,' Slade confirmed, his face serious, a pain there she had never seen before as he remembered. 'All powers of logic deserted me as I searched for you. I knew terror that I might come across you—lifeless.'

It was in that moment that her belief that he did mean it when he said he loved her began to grow in Kimberley. No man could look so haunted, so agonised by the pain of what he was recalling, and not feel as deeply as he had told her he did.

'Oh, Slade!' she cried, and saw the cloud go from his eyes, eyes dark now with emotion as he told her:

'I nearly went out of my mind that day—cursed myself for being too rough on you the night before. You'd given me a lot to think about,' he broke off to tell her. 'I knew after you'd gone to bed that second night that with you so close I wasn't thinking straight. I decided to go to London the next day, I needed to be away from you. With you safely back home the fears I'd had that . . .'

'That I might have ended it all?'

He nodded, his face grim for a moment, then sending her another loving look, he said, 'My fears seemed ridiculous. But when I discovered you kept a supply of tranquillisers, knowing you didn't want a marriage at all, I had to get away to think it out.'

'You came back laden with suitcases,' she remembered.

'With you firmly set on divorce, I decided you'd better start getting used to the idea that I was going to be a permanent fixture.'

'I'm glad,' said Kimberley honestly.

And it was then the control Slade was exerting broke. A groan left him as he pressed her up against his body, his head coming down as his mouth claimed hers. Kimberley hung on tightly, drowning in his love as without reservation her arms went round him and she kissed him back clinging to him.

'My darling, my darling,' Slade murmured, his voice thick with emotion.

'Oh, Slade, I love you so,' Kimberley whispered, tears she couldn't stay swimming in her eyes.

A shuddered breath left him. 'Sweet Kim,' he said hoarsely. 'You have no idea what you've put me through. Wanting you so badly, almost taking you so glad was I to see you that second time I came back from London.'

'Why did you go—that second time?' she asked, but her question then wasn't because she distrusted him. And it showed in her face, delighting Slade as, unable to resist it, he bent and kissed her long and meaningfully.

When at last he drew back, Kimberley's face was showing the delicate hue of aroused womanhood. His hands went to her hair, releasing it from the pins that confined it, the pins scattering unheeded to the floor as a sigh of satisfaction left him before he buried his head in the perfume of her long tresses.

'I adore you, my beloved,' he breathed. And he seemed to have forgotten her question entirely as he led her to a chair and pulled her down on to his lap, his hands caressing, seeming not to mind at all that her fingers strayed to touch his mouth.

He kissed her fingers, looked down at her where she nestled in his arms. He was about to kiss her, when an expression crossed his face as that of a man with a vague recollection of being asked something.

'Er—my second visit to London,' he said, cancelling out what he had been about to do, prepared to do anything that would do away with her slightest worry, 'was purely and simply because I was trying to get you to see me as a husband. To my mind you'd sounded just a touch as though you didn't like the idea of me having—er—extra-marital activities. I thought then it was worth working on.'

'I thought, when you left me without kicking up a fuss—that night you came back—that you might have already . . .' she couldn't finish it.

'There's been no one since I met you, my love,' Slade told her. 'How could there be?—you fill my thoughts. But it was after that night when I went to my solitary bed wondering if I was a fool not to take you as I was aching to, that you told me you didn't know if you still loved Bennet. It was a red letter day for me. I saw then that if I were to gain what I was hoping, then it would be foolhardy of me to rush you. I saw then that with that fine sensitivity you have, the time to adjust you asked for, whether you knew it or not, was what you needed.'

'You've been so patient,' Kimberley sighed, finding joy that she could look at him the love shining in her eyes, and not have to hide it.

'Keep looking at me like that, my darling,' Slade said softly, 'and you'll discover just how impatient a man can be for the woman who holds his heart.'

His longing for her showed as he pulled her close, his hand at her breast, his mouth caressed her eyes, her throat, and finally her mouth. His colour was flushed too when at last he drew back.

She saw his glance go to the bed. Intuitively she knew he didn't care much for her hotel bedroom. Then she saw exactly what he meant by a man being impatient for the woman who held his heart, when softly he groaned, and said:

'Do we have to go back to Bramcote, my darling?'

Her heart so full, Kimberley was having difficulty in thinking clearly. Then she knew her feet had found that firm foothold in the confidence of his love, that she was able to say, and manage to make it sound quite demure:

'I've never seen the inside of your London home.' But a blushed covered her, as she asked, 'Is it very far away?' and she was enchanted by the look he gave her.

'About fifteen minutes,' he replied. 'But I reckon I can do it in ten.'

He kissed her again before he lifted her and stood with her. Once more he held her close to his heart, then as if he needed a moment to ease the arousal of his ardour before they left the hotel, with that way he had of making her laugh at the least expected moment; he let some daylight come between their bodies, and looking deeply into her eyes, said gruffly:

'Come, wife. It's time I made an honest woman of you.'

Harlequin® Plus

THE ORIGIN
OF THE HARLEQUIN EMBLEM

Who is the little fellow sitting within the diamond-shaped emblem that appears on the covers of Harlequin books? He's Harlequin, of course, and he comes to us from the Italian theater of three hundred years ago.

In the sixteenth century, Italian actors formed themselves into traveling troupes known as the commedia dell' arte. Each troupe had the same cast of characters; and one of those characters was Harlequin.

Harlequin's role was that of a servant or valet. It was his job to provide comic relief in the light plays of the company performed for the people of the countryside. Although Harlequin was essentially a clown, his character also contained elements of romance and sadness.

In the plays, Harlequin was required to perform elaborate gymnastic feats. As he teased the other characters, he danced, jumped in the air and walked on stilts. Through the centuries this role evolved into the Harlequin we know today—a jester garbed in a double-pointed hat and a tunic decorated with diamonds.

Harlequin is an ideal character to serve as the symbol for the romance novels our millions of readers so enjoy. His original purpose was to entertain theatrical audiences with tales of exotic places and romantic love. Today he plays a similar role: he is the host who invites millions of women into the world of Harlequin romances.

The bestselling epic saga of the Irish
An intriguing and passionate story that spans 400 years.

FIRST...
The Defiant

Lady Elizabeth Hatton, highborn Englishwoman, was not above using her position to get what she wanted ...and more than anything in the world she wanted Rory O'Donnell, the fiery Irish rebel. But it was an alliance that promised only ruin....

THEN...
The Survivors

Against a turbulent background of political intrigue and royal corruption, the determined, passionate Shanna O'Hara searched for peace in her beloved but troubled Ireland. Meanwhile in England, hot-tempered Brenna Coke fought against a loveless marriage....

Readers rave about Harlequin romance fiction...

"I absolutely adore Harlequin romances! They are fun and relaxing to read, and each book provides a wonderful escape."
—N.E.,* Pacific Palisades, California

"Harlequin is the best in romantic reading."
—K.G., Philadelphia, Pennsylvania

"Harlequin romances give me a whole new outlook on life."
—S.P., Mecosta, Michigan

"My praise for the warmth and adventure your books bring into my life."
—D.F., Hicksville, New York

*Names available on request.